PRAISE FOR JAMES MELVILLE'S
SAYONARA, SWEET AMARYLLIS

"Another fascinating, tightly constructed Japanese detective mystery . . . This evenly paced puzzler is enhanced by the author's ability to intelligently convey the unique tenor and method of Japanese police work."

Booklist

"Hard on the heels of *Death of a Daimyo* comes this satisfying investigation colored in with fine, sure strokes."

The Kirkus Reviews

"Highly polished and carefully put together."

The Times Literary Supplement

"Melville's insouciantly witty, stylish chronicles of crime and punishment in Japan have gained him devoted fans who won't want to miss the latest investigations by Kobe-based inspectors Otani, Kimura, and Noguchi."

Publishers Weekly

Fawcett Crest Books
by James Melville:

THE CHRYSANTHEMUM CHAIN

DEATH OF A DAIMYO

THE NINTH NETSUKE

SAYONARA, SWEET AMARYLLIS

A SORT OF SAMURAI

THE WAGES OF ZEN

SAYONARA, SWEET AMARYLLIS

James Melville

FAWCETT CREST • NEW YORK

A Fawcett Crest Book
Published by Ballantine Books

First published in Great Britain by Martin Secker & Warburg Ltd.

Library of Congress Catalog Card Number: 84-18352

ISBN 0-449-20825-7

This edition published by arrangement with St. Martin's Press, Inc.

Manufactured in the United States of America

First Ballantine Books Edition: July 1987

For Mike and Maitou

Gambatte, ne?

AUTHOR'S NOTE

Hyogo is a real prefecture, and it has a police force. It should be emphasised therefore that all the characters in this story are wholly fictitious and bear no relation to any actual person, living or dead.

甘離々洲さよなら

Chapter 1

There was a wylye ladde . . .

INSPECTOR JIRO KIMURA OF THE HYOGO PREFECTURAL Police Force glanced approvingly in the mirror at his impeccable black bow tie, nestling immaculately on the brilliant white of his shirt. He had tied it himself, having gone to a good deal of trouble to find one of the old kind among the flashy velvet clip-on specimens which abound in the covered Motomachi shopping precinct of Kobe. Well satisfied, as usual, with his appearance, he whipped the snowy napkin over the sleeve of his white cotton jacket, picked up his tray and emerged from the kitchen to serve a fresh load of drinks at the Carradines' farewell party for the Baldwins.

Kimura was no stranger to the higher-priced apartment blocks in which the better-off members of the expatriate business and consular community of Kobe lived, but even he recognised that the Carradines' quarters were of exceptional spaciousness and luxury. There were only four flats in the entire building, which was terraced into the lower slopes of the wooded hills near the venerable Kobe Club, and incorporated a cavernous garage with space not only for cars belonging to residents, but an unusually lavish provision for those of visitors.

Arriving by taxi well before the party was due to begin, Kimura had seen the Carradines' white Rolls-Royce snugly tucked in beyond the Mercedes which he thought must belong to the Spanish couple in the garden flat. There was also a sparkling new Nissan Cedric which Kimura knew was the property of the influential critic and television personality who occupied the second floor with an elegant lady whom Kimura doubted very much was his wife. It was easy to guess from his manner on camera that he was the sort of Japanese who would choose to live among foreigners. Indeed Inspector Kimura would have done so himself had he been able to afford their kind of rent. There was a vacant numbered space in the garage which suggested that the Greek family who had the third floor might be away for the weekend: Kimura could not remember offhand what sort of car they had.

The risk that he might be recognised by one of the guests seemed to have been well calculated. So far as the more important ones were concerned, Kimura felt pretty confident that if any of them had ever had any official dealings with him they might possibly think his face vaguely familiar but would assume that this was because he had been engaged as a waiter at some other party they had attended. All the well-to-do foreigners tended to call on the Kobe Maid Service and Baby-Sitting Agency for part-time help, and the same waiters and waitresses reported for duty fairly regularly on the cocktail circuit.

The real danger was that the Carradines might have

invited one or two single girls from among the junior consular or secretarial staff. There were hardly any expatriate girls employed in this way by the business firms, but several in the various Consulates General, and Kimura was currently involved in a gratifying affair with a Scandinavian vice-consul while disengaging himself with care from an American teacher who seemed to have developed worrying thoughts of marriage. Kimura at forty had not been married and was firmly determined never to abandon his bachelor ways. It would have been unfortunate to the point of calamity if either Ulla or Barbara had turned up, but happily there was no sign of either of them among the chattering crowd in the huge living-room, spilling out onto the balcony of the penthouse apartment with its splendid and expensive view of Kobe Harbour and of the Inland Sea beyond.

It was a perfectly lovely evening. September was always a tricky month to plan a big social occasion, especially in western Japan with its vulnerability to typhoons. One such had in fact skirted Shikoku island to the south three days previously, bringing torrential rain to the whole region, but apart from a landslide in the mountains above the city there had been nothing special to worry about, and the washed and crystalline blue of the sky on the following day had made the downpour seem a very small price to pay. The party had begun at the quite normal hour of six, and still through the open glass doors the last of a fiery ochre sunset could be seen staining the evening sky; there was less humidity in the air than there had been for months.

Mrs Baldwin was holding court in one corner of the living-room, swathed in lace the colour of milky coffee, and the flow of her conversation was maintained as Kimura approached her side and she thrust her almost empty glass in his direction and received in its place a fresh gin and tonic. This was one of the five options available, the others being whisky and water, Campari and soda, beer, and orange juice. Kimura noted that gin seemed to be in fashion that season, since his tray was rapidly denuded of the remaining three or four glasses by others in her vicinity.

". . . it's quite absurd, of course," she was stressing to a small, crushed-looking man who seemed to be trying to attract the attention of someone on the other side of the room, "for them to transfer George just when I'd taken on the Red Cross, the Animal Welfare Chrysanthemum Fayre and everything else. Of course, I've made it quite clear that whatever he decides to do I can't possibly get away before the Extraordinary General Meeting to choose a new President." She snorted briefly and swallowed nearly half her drink before putting down the glass, now decorated with a smear of thick, greasy, bright orange lipstick. Then Mrs Baldwin extended a fat hand, the rings she wore deeply embedded in the pudgy flesh, and grasped the little man's sleeve. "I don't mind telling you that the person they have in mind to succeed me is a most peculiar choice, if you want my opinion. I shall obviously have to come back for the Plum Blossom Ball to see that everything goes properly."

"We shall miss you, Dorothy," the man admitted in an unexpectedly resonant voice. "Wednesday evenings won't be the same."

Mrs Baldwin heaved an ostentatious sigh, and smiled serenely. "One does leave with a teeny sense of having created a—well, would oasis of culture be putting it too boldly? I must admit that the Madrigal Circle is something I am rather proud of. And it's sweet of Patrick and Angela to invite all the members tonight." She paused and reached out for her drink as Kimura moved away. "Even Mr Hagiwara," he heard her add enigmatically, with an air of tried patience.

Armed with his tray, Kimura approached a red-faced, bulky man in outlandish clothes which Kimura identified as Scottish national dress. This man spoke in quaintly accented Japanese, though most of the foreign guests addressed Kimura and the other waiter in English when asking for drinks. There was no need to speak to the two Filipino women who moved about proffering their platters of cocktail sausages on sticks, chicken livers wrapped in bacon, and canapés of one sort and another; and they were indeed largely ignored, by Japanese and foreign guests alike. Kimura himself had a soft spot for all women of any age or nationality, and noted that one of the Filipinas had a deliciously shy, melting smile. She must have been at least his own age, however, and that would never do.

Kimura's English was excellent, and there was not much he failed to understand in the snatches of conversation he overheard as he moved quietly about the room bowing slightly as he accepted empty glasses and offered full ones, with unsatisfactory paper napkins to wrap round them. They soon became soggy and some of the guests managed to shred them absent-mindedly, leaving curious little worms and balls of paper on the lush golden carpet. Kimura, however, had no idea what a Madrigal Circle might be, though he knew that Patrick and Angela were the given names of the host and hostess, who were favoured with beauty as well as wealth.

He was much too professional to forget his role at the party, but was glad of the chance of a good look at Angela Carradine when she clapped her hands for attention and the increasingly noisy general conversation was stilled while she made her announcement. "Now listen everybody,'' she commanded, good humoured but firm. ''No speeches tonight—''

''Shame!'' It was the red-faced Scotsman, on whom Mrs Carradine turned a witheringly sweet smile. ''Dear Fergus, we can always rely on you, can't we? No speeches tonight, but we all know about Dorothy's super work with the Madrigal Circle she founded and guided over—goodness, it must be seven years, from what I hear—and we've asked all the members tonight. Most of them have come, and now we want them to sing for their drinks and nibbles. Clear a place for them and *quiet* everybody. Specially Fergus.''

Kimura gazed hungrily at the gorgeous creature as a ripple of laughter ran round the room and people made way for the members of the Madrigal Circle. Angela Carradine was wearing a low-cut black silk jersey dress which clung lovingly to her, and Kimura reflected that she could only look more edible in a wet T-shirt like the girls on the big posters, in spite or perhaps because of her Amazonian build. Tall as she was, her husband, who was now standing at her side, was taller by a couple of inches, and the pair of them looked like particularly well-dressed advertisements for the English branch of the Californian Grapefruit Growers' Association, so even was their tan, so white their teeth and so assured their place in the sun. The Rolls-Royce in the garage seemed not so much a matter of gilding the lily as an inevitable component of the package.

Gulping inwardly, Kimura moved respectfully towards the wall with the intention of standing unobtrusively to attention during what was evidently to be some sort of musical performance, only to be intercepted by Mrs Baldwin, who deprived Kimura of the last gin and tonic on the tray he had replenished several times in the past half hour, and carried it with her as she joined the group now beginning to shuffle about and clear their throats self-consciously. "A little tholubric . . . thoracic lubricant in order," she announced with a smile whose brightness was beginning to have a glazed quality. "Farewell performance, after all . . ." Her speech was slurred and she was manifestly tipsier than any of those around her.

Kimura counted ten in all, of whom four were Japanese. Since only one of these was male, Kimura concluded that he must be the Mr Hagiwara about whom Mrs Baldwin had sounded dubious earlier. He was certainly an odd-looking man, gangling and awkward, and with a face which seemed to cave in. He stood at one end, next to the little man with the loud voice. Two more foreign men completed the male voice section, one elderly with bright blue eyes and the other much younger, lurking behind a huge brown beard. Then came two middle-aged Japanese ladies, then Mrs Baldwin and next to her a younger Japanese woman with an interesting intelligent face. Two more foreign ladies completed the line-up, one a good deal taller than the other but neither remarkable except for the fact that the small dark one looked uncertain and referred to sheet music, unlike the other singers.

Mrs Baldwin drained her glass with impressive speed and handed it imperiously to the Japanese girl beside her, then fished in her beaded jet evening bag and produced a tuning fork, which she struck against a fine lacquer box on an occasional table nearby. Even Kimura winced, and he was no connoisseur of such things. Holding the tuning fork to her ear, her eyes closed and swaying a little, Mrs Baldwin uttered a nasal sound which was picked up by the ladies beside her, then in a rumbling assortment of variations by the four men. Mr Hagiwara's eyes were closed also as he groaned, and the little man at his side nudged him into silence as Mrs Baldwin waved a pudgy hand, then gave a downbeat:

> "It was a lover and his lasse
> With a haye, with a hoe and a haye nonie no,
> That o'er the green corne fields did passe
> In spring time, the onley prettie ring time,
> When Birds do sing, haye ding a ding a ding,
> Sweete lovers love the spring."

Kimura had no ear for music either, but the reedy warblings of the oddly assorted group sounded particularly unattractive to him. The song or whatever it was seemed to go on for ever, and he couldn't make head or tail of the words. Most of the singers stayed more or less together, though Mr Hagiwara finished each of what seemed to be four repetitions of the piece half a second or so later than the others, drawing attention to his own voice, which had a phlegmy quality not unlike that of the narrators of the *bunraku* puppet plays Kimura had enjoyed once in Osaka far more than he had expected to.

A small murmur of conversation developed as the singing wore on, and during the half-hearted applause which followed when it was finally over Kimura noticed Angela Carradine wagging an admonitory finger in the direction of the offenders. It seemed, therefore, that there was more to come. Some sort of consultation was taking place among the singers and soon reached a conclusion with much nodding of heads. Mrs Baldwin announced it.

"Snot specially suitable," she said, then giggled briefly and dabbed her mouth dry again with the back of the hand in which she still held the tuning fork. "Buss very lovely maggle." She was clearly now very drunk indeed, and the little man next to Mr Hagiwara took the tuning fork from her and struck it on the sole of his shoe. The same curious humming and shuffling of feet ensued, then the voices were again upraised.

"Come heavy sleepe, the Image of true death:
And close up . . ."

Everyone except Mr Hagiwara stopped singing at about the same time. Eyes closed, he alone completed the line—". . . close up these my weary weeping eyes Whose spring of tears doth stop my vitall breath . . ." Then he too blinked and fell uneasily silent as those nearest to her clustered round the fallen Dorothy Baldwin.

The Scotsman called Fergus was the first to break the resulting hush. "Poor old Dot," he boomed. "One over the eight. Better after a wee bit of shut-eye." Like all Japanese, Kimura was both familiar with and tolerant of public drunkenness though it was extremely rare in a woman of the respectable classes. He watched quietly as a previously unidentified man who must be George Baldwin bustled over and with the aid of Angela Carradine hauled his wife first into an armchair and from there to an upright position. At this point they were joined by Patrick Carradine, who shouldered his way roughly through those in his way, his face grim and set. Joining George Baldwin, who held his wife sagging against him with one of her arms pulled round his neck and his own free arm round her thick waist, Carradine helped him to half drag, half carry her into what was obviously a bedroom, preceded by Mrs Carradine.

Baldwin would, Kimura judged, have been an unimpressive man even if viewed in much more favourable circumstances. It was always difficult to judge the age of foreigners, but he seemed to be in the mid-fifties. He had sparse sandy hair plastered across a pink scalp, and his glasses had not only been knocked off centre by his efforts, but were partly steamed over. "Dear oh dear," he puffed to nobody in particular. "Passed out cold. Too much excitement . . ." Then the door closed behind the little group and within a minute or so the party was back in almost full swing.

Kimura overheard no particular references to the incident as he circulated with yet another loaded tray, except when one man helped himself to a whisky and water and as he did so remarked to his companion "At least it put a stop to those bloody madrigals or whatever the hell they are. They'd probably still be at it otherwise."

Kimura then moved out to the balcony, collecting empty glasses from where they had been carelessly left about on the parapet. The few people out there were mostly Japanese, two of the ladies in expensive silk kimonos. Since the balcony was illuminated with carefully placed Japanese paper lanterns, the total effect was much more mysteriously oriental than the brightly Western atmosphere of the opulently furnished living room with its costly reproduction French furniture, oil paintings on the fabric covered walls, and chandelier lighting. The lacquer box to which Mrs Baldwin had done violence with her tuning fork was one of the few Japanese touches in the room, along with a woodblock print which Kimura failed to recognise as being from an original Utamaro edition, and a reproduction Kano screen in rich greens and golds which partially concealed the entrance to the kitchen.

It was a good twenty minutes later and Kimura was not far from the bedroom door when it opened again and Carradine emerged, his face drawn and the suntan looking as though it had come out of a bottle. Conversation died away as people became infected by his expression, and he had no need to clap for silence. "I'm frightfully sorry, friends," he said, his voice easy and unforced in spite of tension in his posture. "I think perhaps we'd better call it a day. I'm afraid Dorothy's not at all well and we shall have to have an ambulance. In fact I've phoned already. I think it might simplify things if you'd accept our apologies and be making your way . . ."

There was a general murmur of consternation and a distinct jam built up in the entrance hallway as people began to leave. Fortunately at that time of the year there were few coats and bags to be reclaimed, and most of the trouble was caused by the Japanese guests who found themselves unable to leave without formal bows and expressions of appreciation to Mr Carradine, as well as urgent requests to be remembered to Mrs Carradine, not to mention Mr and Mrs Baldwin.

Carradine dealt with them abstractedly but courteously, the centre of a whirlpool round which the Western guests swirled and eddied as they slipped away with much less fuss. Mr Hagiwara was the most troublesome, being apparently determined to remain and render assistance until Carradine grasped him roughly by the arm and virtually propelled him out of the front door.

In spite of the confusion Kimura was able to exchange no more than a few words with the other waiter as they busied themselves emptying ashtrays and collecting trayloads of glasses for the Filipino maids to deal with in the big, well-equipped kitchen. Kimura had been both surprised and pleased by the way Detective Patrolman Migishima had adjusted during the two or three months his name had been on the books of the Kobe Maid Service and Baby-Sitting Agency. Marriage seemed to have done him good, and though he was too bulky to slide about as unobtrusively as a good waiter should, when Kimura had contrived to be present as a guest on one occasion when Migishima was on duty in his undercover capacity, his assistant had managed to give him a drink without allowing a flicker of recognition to pass between them.

The wailing of an ambulance siren drifted through the open balcony windows and grew louder till the noise stopped abruptly. A few minutes later two men in white coats appeared at the door carrying a stretcher, followed by another carrying portable emergency oxygen apparatus. Patrick Carradine led them towards the bedroom, thanking them in fluent and idiomatic Japanese for their prompt arrival as he did so. Bringing up the rear of the little procession was a uniformed policeman with a walkie-talkie radio in his hand. He remained in the living-room, a look of eager interest on his face.

Kimura tightened his lips and managed to catch Migishima's eyes. He shook his head almost imperceptibly and Migishima nodded briefly back. Neither of them had ever consciously set eyes on their uniformed colleague before, but determined as he was to sustain his role Kimura found it difficult to do so when the patrolman approached and spoke to him in unvarnished, almost rudely colloquial language. Suppressing an urgent desire to instruct the man to mind his manners, Kimura somehow managed to remain a waiter as he politely addressed the man as *o-mawari-san* and briefly explained that one of the guests at the party had been taken ill.

"Ill, or pissed?" the patrolman demanded, then, without waiting for a reply, "Do you work here full-time?"

At that moment the ambulance men came out of the

bedroom carrying the stretcher. A crisp, fresh white sheet was drawn up over the head of the bulky form of Mrs Baldwin, and one of the Filipinas who was standing in the open doorway to the kitchen sucked in her breath sharply and crossed herself. ''Dead, is she?'' barked the policeman officiously and unnecessarily, and one of the ambulance men nodded curtly as they passed him. ''I shall have to take some statements,'' he went on with relish as the Carradines and Mr Baldwin came out of the bedroom.

Baldwin's face was blotched and he looked dazed. Angela Carradine's exuberant radiance seemed to have disappeared entirely, and even her formerly glossy hair looked limp and lifeless. Patrick Carradine walked like an automaton as all three followed the stretcher bearers as they awkwardly negotiated the service stairs with their burden. Last of all went the man with the oxygen gear, and he used the lift.

The flat was now deserted except for the maids, Kimura and Migishima, and the local patrolman. He produced his notebook, looked round for a comfortable chair and prepared to enjoy himself. ''Right,'' he announced. ''For a start I shall want all your names and addresses . . .''

Chapter 2

If ever haples woman . . .

"So, TO CUT A LONG STORY SHORT, I HAD TO GO to the Ikuta Divisional Headquarters and sort it out myself," said Superintendent Tetsuo Otani to his wife Hanae after he had given the waitress their order. They were in a small restaurant in the underground shopping complex at the central Umeda Station in Osaka. Normally Hanae did her more serious shopping in Kobe, but the Hankyu Department Store was holding a special sale of high-class menswear, and she had persuaded her husband that it was time he bought a new suit.

"But why was Mr Kimura there in the first place?" she enquired, intrigued. Otani took a pair of wooden chopsticks from the bamboo holder on the table between them and pulled them apart. They were of the cheap kind which often fail to separate neatly, and he scowled at the result of his efforts before trying another pair with more success. Then he looked at Hanae, who was wearing a kimono he particularly liked, in a deep russet shade which set off her smooth skin and lustrous black hair. Hanae made no particular effort to disguise her age, but in her mid-forties took good care of herself, and to Otani's eyes looked a good deal more attractive than the women who modelled fashions for mature ladies in the big glossy magazines Hanae bought and which he leafed through from time to time.

"It goes back nearly a year," he said at last, just as the waitress brought their food. He had a big bowl of buckwheat noodles in broth, surmounted by pieces of lightly poached duck breast, and tipped the contents of the separate small dish of sliced spring onion on top. Hanae had chosen a more elegant lunch of cold cooked noodles in three shallow lacquer boxes one on top of the other, with a bowl of seasoned sauce to dip them in. "Kimura has always had the general job of keeping an eye on the foreigners, of course. The Europeans and Americans and so on. Some of the Indians too, but the Chinese and the Koreans are in a different category, obviously."

Hanae nodded. It was indeed obvious to her that the Koreans and Chinese in Kobe with their complicated legal status would have to be treated as special cases. Many of them were second, third or even fourth generation residents who had never been outside Japan and never would go, for fear of being refused a re-entry visa. After Nagasaki and Yokohama, Kobe had the biggest community of Chinese in Japan. Hanae enjoyed exploring the mysteries of the stocks in the speciality groceries they ran, and sometimes bought amazingly cheap jam and tinned foods from them.

"Although his main responsibility is drug control, Ninja Noguchi takes care of anything serious involving those communities." Hanae nodded again. She knew not only that Inspector Noguchi had an unparalleled range of contacts in the underworld at large, but that quite a lot of the minor executive side of organised crime was in the hands of the Koreans. Although most of them spoke no language but Japanese, they were as precise a category of aliens as if they had been physically as conspicuous as Swedes or African pigmies.

Otani picked up his bowl and drank some of the broth from it, then put it down and sprinkled some seven-flavour spice into it from the shaker on the table. "It works out very well usually," he went on. "As a matter of fact most drug pushers seem to be Koreans anyway, and the occasional Westerner who gets into that kind of trouble is usually operating on his own."

Otani was wearing one of his ordinary dark suits in honour of their Sunday visit to town, especially as they were going to the superior men's clothing department, and now rummaged through a wallet he took out from an inside pocket and produced a folded sheet of paper. He opened his mouth to read something from it to Hanae, then thought better of it and put the paper away again. He smiled at her. "I can't pronounce these foreign names anyway," he said. "Well, a long time ago now Ninja came on something out of the ordinary. A lead that seemed to suggest that a new wholesaler had appeared in this area. Someone with quite different channels of supply from usual. Ninja took it as far as he could, then brought Kimura in when the trail seemed to lead to a respectable foreigner—I mean a Westerner. Kimura hit on the idea that a good way to find out if there's any gossip about him among the *gaijin* community would be to put an undercover man into the regular group of parttime waiters who are in and out of their homes all the time. Did you realise that these people give *parties* in their houses?" Otani sighed deeply and shook his head in disbelief at his own words. Even Hanae, who was less unsympathetic to Western ways than her husband, found it difficult to understand why any sensitive person should want a crowd of casual acquaintances invading a private residence when there were perfectly good restaurants and hotels available to entertain in.

She had finished her noodles while Otani was speaking and now reached for the bill as he polished off the last of his own meal and the remains of the small bottle of beer he had ordered for himself. It was understood that the cost of their lunch would come from the housekeeping budget, even though, unlike a good many Japanese wives, Hanae was quite generous in the amount of pocket money she gave her husband back from the salary packet he handed over to her intact each month. They left the crowded little restaurant, outside which several potential customers were waiting for tables, with Otani hanging about for a minute while Hanae settled up at the cash desk before joining him. He spoke more freely when they joined the anonymous crowd flowing steadily towards the main concourse.

"Well, you know Kimura," Otani said. "He gave the job to the Migishima boy, then decided he could do it better himself. It's true that Migishima doesn't speak English nearly so well as Kimura, though Kimura tells me he's making very good progress. That new wife of his has certainly made a difference."

"Has she stayed in the police force?" Hanae had meant to ask for some time, having liked the look of both Detective Patrolman Migishima and his bride when meeting them for the first time at their wedding reception.

"So far she has," Otani replied, pointing in the direction they needed to go for the best approach to the

Hankyu Department Store. "It seems she's applied for a transfer to the criminal investigation section. Inspector Sakamoto is making difficulties about taking on a married woman, though."

Their conversation lapsed as they made their way up the stairs and into the hazy sunshine at street level, Hanae being slowed down somewhat by the restricting folds of her kimono. "Not too hot for you?" enquired Otani, suddenly sticky himself after the air-conditioning of the underground shopping centre. Hanae shook her head. It was in any case only a short walk to the department store, crowded as always on a Sunday but also air-conditioned. "I seem to be talking a lot more to you nowadays about police business," Otani went on thoughtfully. "Getting indiscreet in my old age. It's a good thing you're not a gossip too."

Hanae glanced at him with a hint of a smile. "I'm sure nobody was listening in the restaurant," she reassured him. "It was much too noisy. And you know I never talk to anyone else about your work. What you haven't said is whether Mr Kimura and Mr Migishima found out anything interesting."

They had arrived at the main entrance to the department store and made their way inside, past the girl in the latest uniform, a fitted suit in an unhappy shade of yellow, with white gloves and a kind of sailor hat, who murmured an unceasing stream of phrases of welcome in ridiculously refined language. Another, similarly kitted out, stood at the foot of the escalator with a soft cloth with which she dusted the handrail, bowing from time to time as customers streamed past her unseeingly. "Yes and no," said Otani judiciously as they disembarked at the gentlemen's wear department. "I'd call a murder pretty interesting, myself." Otani was an avid reader of detective stories, preferring translations of those written in the West. He was already thinking of Kimura's latest case as 'Death in Close Harmony', or perhaps 'The Case of the Interrupted Cadence', being more musical than his subordinate.

Otani had been in very good spirits previously, but gloom now fell upon him as he faced the ordeal ahead. Rack upon rack of suits stretched out in an infinity of choice, and the looks on the faces both of Hanae and of the young salesman who came bustling up to attend to them made it perfectly clear that a purchase was inevitable. Apart from his winter and summer uniforms and his formal Japanese dress, the heavy black silk of the *haori* bearing the Otani family crest in white in the prescribed five places, Otani possessed four more or less identical business suits, and a tweed sports jacket with a pair of grey slacks which in his opinion went with it. For the life of him he could see no point in adding to his wardrobe and his swarthy face took on a mulish expression as he allowed himself to be inserted into three jackets in succession. However, he watched Hanae carefully and came to the conclusion that of the three she liked the dark blue best, so leaving her holding his old jacket he took the proffered trousers and, removing his shoes as he did so, stepped into the tiny curtained cubicle indicated by the salesman to try them on.

Mercifully, they fitted him reasonably well, and the remainder of the transaction was completed within a few minutes. Seventy-five thousand yen seemed rather a lot of money, but Hanae had warned him that he ought to take a hundred thousand with him, so perhaps it could have been worse. Otani had recently discovered that Kimura had acquired a personal cheque book; a rare thing in Japan where most transactions are cash, even when involving very large sums. He and Hanae had no intention of penetrating such arcane financial mysteries, and usually kept the equivalent of half a month's salary lying about in cash at home. One never knew when a bill collector might turn up demanding settlement on the spot.

The next thing was a new pair of shoes and a new tie, and Otani was a bundle of nerves by the time they had been selected and bought. He agreed readily enough when Hanae suggested they might go to the specialist food department to see if they could find something interesting for supper. There seemed as they approached it to be some kind of special promotion going on. Over the normal background music played throughout the store and interspersed with announcements about lost children and reminders that the sales were now in full swing, Otani thought he could hear the strains of Hawaiian guitars. His impression was confirmed as they came into range and saw that a palm-roofed stage had been set up in a corner of the huge area devoted to foodstuffs, just beyond the array of imported wines and spirits.

A boldly-lettered banner announced astonishing bargains in macadamia nuts and pineapples, but this was not what most of the considerable crowd were looking at. The syrupy guitar music was taped, but the three girls undulating on the stage in grass skirts over almost unnecessarily modest pink knickers with bandeaus of similar material covering their breasts were live enough. They kept together pretty well, the ropes of plastic flowers round their necks swaying in unison as they moved, and Hanae scrutinised them with mild interest. The one on the right was almost certainly Japanese, even though she had made up the exposed areas of her body so as to approximate to the natural honey colour of her two companions. Though their facial features were coarser than those of the third girl, they had much more lithe and sensual-looking bodies.

Hanae cast a sidelong glance at her husband, who was gazing at the spectacle with every appearance of scholarly concentration, the bag containing his new suit dangling from one hand, the separately packed shoes and tie from the other. "Enjoying yourself?" she enquired, a hint of tartness in her voice.

Otani grinned. "Bored, actually," he claimed innocently. "My only interest is to find out what 'macadamia nuts' are." They moved on and he waited patiently while Hanae chose a few odds and ends, then suggested that they might as well look at the exhibition in the top floor gallery.

This was of deceptively simple pieces by one of the most famous living potters, and the contrast in mood with the display of Hawaiian dancing below could scarcely have been more marked. Department store directors have been advised by their researchers that silence must at all costs be avoided, but some obstinate residue of sensitivity had prompted someone in authority to insist that in this area at least the music from the concealed loudspeaker system should be that of the Japanese bamboo flute, weaving a heartbreaking skein of sound which seemed to settle almost visibly round the dull browns and tranquil blues and greens of the tea-bowls and vases, many of them displayed on squares of silk placed on top of the simple but beautifully fashioned plain wooden Coxes in which they were intended to be kept when not in use. Each of these bore in flowing black brushed calligraphy the name of the piece and a statement of its provenance, with the red seal of the potter providing the only touch of bright colour.

"I like that one," said Hanae wistfully, indicating a tea-bowl of seemingly unremarkable appearance. It was not until one looked for a second time that the fiery underglaze seemed to glow through the predominantly dun colour of the surface.

Otani bent to inspect the piece. "Some sort of iron compound in the glaze, by the look of it . . ." He screwed up his eyes and then took out his glasses from an inner pocket and put them on to read the details on the small white card. It took a few moments to decipher the price, written as it was in the archaic Chinese style normally reserved for legal documents. Then he straightened up slowly and smiled ruefully at Hanae. "Yes, it's beautiful," he agreed. "At half a year's salary it ought to be."

They moved on companionably, speculating briefly but without particular resentment about the sort of person who could afford to spend millions of yen on a piece of pottery. It was Hanae who pointed out that Europeans might well spend as much or more on a sketch dashed off by Picasso in far less time than the potter had devoted to fashioning the bowl. Otani had never heard of Picasso but remembered his opposite number in the Kyoto Prefectural Police telling him of a spectacular theft of a famous French painting from an exhibition in Kyoto, as a result of which the director of the museum had committed suicide, so he was able to follow Hanae's drift.

It was not until they left the suburban electric train at Rokko Station and were walking up the steep streets towards the old house in which they lived and in which Otani had been brought up that Hanae again raised the subject of the foreigner whom Kimura and Migishima had been keeping under observation. "Did you mean that you think this foreign man murdered the lady at the party?"

Since Hanae had immediately beforehand been talking about the impending birthday of their only grandchild, it took Otani a moment to make the mental jump back to police business. ''It would be tempting to think along those lines,'' he admitted as they turned into the last street of houses before the road petered out into the footpaths which criss-crossed the shaggy and precipitous slopes of Mount Rokko.

Then Otani fell silent, and from previous experience Hanae judged that she would get nothing further from him at that stage. He remained uncommunicative for some time after they reached home, and scarcely noticed as Hanae unwrapped his suit and bore it away upstairs to put with the others. When he did emerge from his reverie he talked to Hanae cheerfully about everyday things, only part of his mind concerned with the following day's conference at police headquarters. It had occurred to him that the murderer might have claimed the wrong victim, and he was wondering whether to mention the possibility to Kimura.

Chapter 3

Musing

"NO DOUBT WHATEVER," KIMURA CONCLUDED decisively. Otani stirred in his chair, reached forward and sipped thoughtfully from the handleless cup of green tea which had been resting on its little lacquer saucer on the low table before him. As usual, Noguchi had left his own untouched, but Kimura had drunk half of his for the sake of politeness. It was only Otani who regularly poured himself a second or third cup from the old tin kettle brought in by his clerk.

The year was not yet sufficiently advanced for the sunshine to come directly into Otani's office on the second floor of the old building which housed the headquarters of the Hyogo Prefectural Police Force, but the view of brilliant blue sky through the windows was a cheering sight, and there was a brightness in the room which showed up the general seediness of its decor and furnishings in a kindly rather than accusing sort of way.

There were divisional headquarters buildings here and there in Otani's enormous domain which were much more modern and were equipped with the latest in electronic gadgetry, and even in this rambling brick-built headquarters there were rooms where young technicians in glasses brooded over machines whose purpose Otani could only guess at.

His own office, however, was much as it had been when he first moved in several years before, relishing at the time the thought that he was probably one of the very last of the old-style prefectural commanders who would be allowed to stay put until retirement, with personal rights preserved in spite of the new National Police Agency policy of uprooting senior officers every few years and dumping them in some completely unfamiliar environment. Perhaps it served as a safeguard against corruption, but as a man of the Kansai area of western Japan born and bred, Otani was relieved that he could look forward to putting in the remaining years of his service among people whose ways he understood, whose comfortable accents fell familiarly on his ears; and above all with the assistance of his two closest associates, Kimura and Noguchi. No doubt Kimura would be delighted if the Public Safety Commission could persuade the prefectural government to put up the money to replace the shabby building, which really did look more like an old-fashioned high school than the headquarters of the third largest police force in Japan, but Otani had no doubt that Noguchi shared his own contentment with the place. He looked across at him.

"What do you think, Ninja?"

Inspector Noguchi was not a particularly tall man, but he had a massive aura. When settled in the easy-chair he always occupied during their conferences, he seemed to become part of it, and when he did move the effect was as if some monstrous creature had begun to stir in the mud in the depths of the ocean. One eyelid opened fractionally, and a beefy hand moved slowly up the majestic belly and rasped dryly across the stubbly crags and ravines of Noguchi's face. "Possible," he eventually conceded. He hated agreeing with Kimura about anything.

Kimura beamed delightedly. He had recently decided to change his image again, and instead of sporting the Italian sweater and cashmere jacket he had invested in, before the hot weather set in, with the idea of wearing them in the autumn, he was nattily dressed in a new grey slimline suit he had bought from Brooks Brothers' expensive store in Tokyo. Barbara, his American mistress, had reflected aloud that the preppy look as favoured by the VicePresident of the United States might become him, and he was more than pleased with the result himself. Although he had no need of glasses, he was contemplating getting some horn-rims with plain glass in the near future.

"It's not as if the symptoms in themselves are all that unusual," he pointed out eagerly. "We all know that on average up to a dozen people a year die of *fugu* fish poisoning in Japan, and nearly always in one or another of the big cities. The main hospitals in Osaka and here in Kobe get cases often enough to recognise them. The reason they didn't come to the conclusion sooner is that in their experience it's always been well known that the victim had been eating *fugu*. Nor is it the first time somebody's been deliberately poisoned with it. Is it, Ninja?"

This time Noguchi nodded his bullet head with the cruelly cropped iron-grey hair in reluctant assent. "Seven, maybe eight years ago. Remember it well. Little restaurant down by the harbour. Cook had a proper licence to serve *fugu*. But he was the one who got killed.

Wife put a bit of liver in his stew. Fancied the mate off a Kyushu coaster. Probably got away with it if the silly cow hadn't talked in her sleep.'' It was a long speech for Noguchi, and he subsided in apparent exhaustion.

''I've never understood what people see in it,'' Otani said with a hint of irritation. ''Ugly creatures in my opinion, though I'll admit the flesh looks pretty when they slice it thin enough to see through. Tastes very boring, though. And just because people will insist on eating it the local authorities have to maintain this elaborate business of inspecting and licensing every blowfish restaurant in the country because the wretched stuff is so dangerous.''

''Ah, but that's the whole point, Chief,'' Kimura insisted. ''People like a bit of excitement. There's always the faint possibility of feeling your lips go numb and realising you've got perhaps only half an hour left . . .''

''Not much chance of your lips going numb, Kimura. Might be worth a try though.'' Noguchi seldom insulted Kimura with such comparative elegance, and Otani inferred that he was in general sympathy with Kimura's line of thinking.

The popularity of the delicate white flesh of the blowfish was indeed a fact of life, and the risks attendant upon eating it were thoroughly well known to practically every Japanese. The official licence to prepare and serve the fish for public consumption was invariably displayed in a prominent place in every *fugu* restaurant, even the smallest and cheapest establishments where it was generally offered in the form of a kind of stew, a far cry from the up-market places Otani had in mind, where customers were invited to admire a huge shallow platter of delicate green celadon ware or other fine ceramic upon which tissue-thin slices of the fish were arranged like the petals of some exotic flower, to be eaten raw as *sashimi*.The traditional sign of such restaurants is a whole dried and inflated *fugu*,pop-eyed and choleric, hanging outside the doorway and sometimes even illuminated eerily from within.

It is in the cleaning of the fish that the skill of the cook is most crucial, for the creature's internal organs contain the highly toxic substance tetradotoxin, one of the fastest-acting poisons occurring in nature. One slip of the knife, and the flesh can become instantly but invisibly contaminated, with generally fatal results for the eater. Otani had read Kimura's report on the circumstances surrounding the death of the foreign woman with close attention, and needless to say had been struck by the findings of the pathologist that there was unmistakable evidence of tetradotoxin poisoning.

"Yes, well, I suppose that might partly account for it," he said to Kimura, who had opened his mouth to reply to Noguchi's sally but thought better of it. "And I accept that the pathologist must be presumed to know his job. The question for you seems to be to work out how the stuff was administered to the woman, by whom and why. Simple for a man like you, Kimura-kun. Only about fifty or sixty suspects, I think you said? I should start with the waiters if I were you."

Kimura glanced warily at his superior. Otani in a quietly sarcastic mood was at his most formidable, and Kimura had not forgotten the twist at the corner of Otani's mouth that evening as he had looked from himself to Migishima and nodded slowly as they stood captive in their white jackets and bow ties in the office of the Divisional Inspector at the Ikuta police station. On that occasion Otani had assured the incredulous Inspector in loyally neutral tones that the two men were indeed respectively the head of the Foreign Affairs Section and one of his assistants.

He had even gone on to point out that it was not unreasonable that they had no identification on their persons, since the officious patrolman had hustled them away from the scene of the party without giving them the chance to retrieve their ordinary clothes from the maid's room in which they had changed before beginning their duties. Only Kimura knew him well enough to realise at the time with morose certitude that Otani was enjoying himself hugely and storing up every little detail of the tableau for future reference in their dealings with each other. This was no doubt the first of many not very subtle digs of the kind Kimura found harder by far to handle than Otani's occasional royal explosions of fury. He decided to face it out.

"Obviously Migishima and I were in a position to see what was going on, and we pooled our recollections of the people who had been in contact with the woman. We ruled out the two Filipino maids in the kitchen—"

"Why? How do you know they were Filipino?"

Kimura gaped. "Of course they were. I mean, it was quite obvious. We spoke to them: they could hardly understand even simple Japanese . . . and one of them made a Catholic sign when she realised Mrs Baldwin was dead . . ."

"Go on." Otani's voice was level and inexpressive.

"We ruled them out anyway because of course they couldn't possibly arrange for any particular guest to take one particular canapé."

"What's a *kanape*?"

Otani's question seemed to be guileless, and Kimura hastened to describe the various bits and pieces of food on offer at the party. "It's a French word," he concluded airily.

"Oh, you mean *odoboru*," said Otani. "Why didn't you say so, instead of showing off your foreign words?"

"*Hors d'oeuvres*, yes," Kimura assented, pronouncing the words correctly and with a heavy irony which was completely lost on Otani.

"Needless to say, *fugu* is never served in this way, but it would be a fairly easy matter to add a fragment of tainted *fugu* to one of the fish-spread pieces of toast. No way of seeing it got to the right person, though. The forensic lab suggested that it would also be possible to produce a highly toxic and concentrated liquid by boiling up *fugu* offal. Alcohol would mask the taste, and you'd only need a few drops . . . same problem of delivery though."

Kimura sat back and crossed his legs, carefully adjusting the crease of his trousers. The waistcoat of his new suit was a little tight, and it was uncomfortable leaning forward. "Actually, since tetradotoxin acts so fast, we can narrow the question 'Who?' down to well below the fifty or sixty people at the party. People formed little groups and stayed together for some time. Both Migishima and I recall that she didn't move far from one spot for well over half an hour, and when the singing began the others moved across to her. At the moment we're concentrating on the choir or whatever it is."

"So far it has been assumed by everyone that it's simple food poisoning, right? You'll have to be careful if you're really determined to treat it as a case of murder." Notwithstanding the relish with which he had spoken to Hanae of murder, from the time when Kimura had first come to him excitedly and sketched out his theory, Otani had wondered whether it was on the whole worth starting such a chancy and potentially troublesome hare.

"I wouldn't have asked to see you this morning if I hadn't been so sure."

Once in a while Kimura managed to make a simple, convincing statement which clearly came from the heart, and when he did so Otani took him seriously. "Very well," he agreed. "Proceed on those lines. All the same, I see no need for publicising our suspicions. Do all you can first without direct questioning. You'll have to look into the question of motive first. It's all very well to accept that she died of *fugu* poisoning and that the only way to account for it is by assuming that somebody deliberately brought the poison to the party and put it into her food or drink. You yourself agree that it seems a very hit-or-miss way of committing a murder, even though on the other hand the chances of its being recognised as such were on the thin side. Before you can convince me that someone intended to kill this woman you'll have to come up with some sort of reason. How old was she, did you say?"

Kimura opened a manila folder which he had put on the shiny brown linoleum floor. The surface was cracked and here and there the hessian backing showed through, but Otani had resisted suggestions that he should have it replaced by the new-style vinyl tiles. The gloomy colour suited the painting which hung on the wall beside the filing cabinet and whose origins were shrouded in mystery. This depicted an animal probably intended to be a stag, but the background was certainly not the park surrounding the Kasuga Shrine in Nara, which was the only place Otani had ever seen such a creature. It was mountainous, and looked un-Japanese. They occasionally speculated about it, and Kimura clung to the view that the setting was Swiss. Noguchi when pressed thought it might be Nagano Prefecture, but Otani had come round to a theory first propounded by Migishima when he had acted temporarily as his confidential clerk, to the effect that it was a place called Scotland, apparently and confusingly located in England.

Having selected one of a number of sheets of paper from the folder, Kimura cleared his throat noisily and began to read aloud. "Baldwin, Dorothy Ursula. Born April 19, 1928 in Bromley, near London, England. That's the third year of Showa," he added hurriedly as Otani produced a pocket diary and began to look up the table of year equivalents. "Family name before marriage was Ridley. Married in 1953—Showa 28—to Baldwin, George Arthur. One adult son, married and living in New Zealand."

Otani finished the last of his cup of tea and grimaced briefly at its bitterness. "Now why would anyone want to kill a married woman in her fifties? Hardly love trouble at that age. Did you get the impression she still took an interest in the opposite sex, Kimura?" Otani's tone was dreamy and he was off down a side turning before Kimura had a chance to reply. "Or the husband. Now that's much more likely," he went on, his imagination fed by countless *krimi* plots. "I understand divorce is much harder to come by in Europe than here. Husband takes a mistress, even falls in love with her, wife refuses divorce, so he decides to kill her. Or the mistress does . . . was he paying attention to any other woman at the party, Kimura? No, of course that's the last thing he'd do. Let's try another approach. Was he very obviously *ignoring* any particular woman? That's often a sure sign, you know . . ."

Eventually Otani came down to earth, sat up straight and looked at the other two. Kimura was studiously examining his fingernails, while Noguchi seemed sunk in a profound torpor, except that one eye was focused on him. Suddenly self-conscious, Otani coughed, then there was silence for several seconds. Finally Noguchi grunted, and offered a view. "Leave all that stuff to Kimura," he advised. "Not too easy to get hold of *fugu*. Find your man that way most likely."

Kimura perked up. "True," he said quickly. "It's not for sale at ordinary fishmongers, of course You can only get it at the central wholesale market, and by showing your licence. In theory. What actually happens is that the licensed restaurants have a regular order with one of the few authorised dealers."

Otani was quite intrigued by this information. "How did you find that out?" he enquired.

It was now Kimura's turn to look embarrassed, and he avoided Noguchi's basilisk eye as he replied. "Actually, Ninja told me," he admitted. "Most of the cheaper *fugu* restaurants are operated by Koreans, and Ninja's the expert on them."

"I see. Well, that's quite useful as far as it goes, but it seems to open up a great many leads. Why, there must be dozens of those little *fugu* places in Kobe." Otani was interested, but not caught up to the extent of involving himself personally in the investigation. He, like Kimura, was well content to leave matters concerning the Korean community to Noguchi, who not only seemed not to object to their company, but was even rumoured to have a number of cronies among them. After all the years of their association, Otani still knew nothing about Noguchi's private life, and had no idea where he lived. It would have been simple enough to discover the address which went with the telephone number Otani had in his notebook for use if he needed to contact Noguchi urgently in his off-duty hours, but he never bothered to do so. On the handful of occasions when he had called the number and left a message with the uncommunicative man who answered, Noguchi had always called back within a matter of minutes.

There was something about Noguchi which seemed to guard him against personal speculation, and it was almost as though all his colleagues joined in an unconscious conspiracy to endorse and sustain the reputation which had earned him the nickname of 'Ninja'. This dated from the beginning of the rash of television serials about the highly skilled spies and assassins of the middle ages who formed a guild of specialists, half thug, half magician, for hire to any local warlord who sought to further his interests by clandestine means. So superstitiously terrified were the common people by tales of their exploits that the *ninja* were believed to be masters of the occult arts, including that of becoming invisible at will.

Certainly Noguchi had an uncanny knack of losing himself in the seedy alleys and cheap amusement quarters of the unfashionable parts of Kobe, and there was not much doubt about his pride in the nickname originally conferred on him in court by an outraged gangster. To probe into his ways would border on the sacrilegious, and his brother officers treated him with cautious respect as a kind of specialist consultant, without enquiring into the methods by which he came by the fund of information he possessed. Only Otani himself ever called Noguchi to account for anything he did, and that very rarely indeed.

"What do you think, Ninja?" he now enquired.

The second eye opened and Noguchi raised his head slowly, like a tortoise emerging from hibernation. "I'll give Kimura a hand," he rumbled. "Got some ideas."

He seemed disinclined to elaborate on what they might be, and Otani judged the conference to be over. "Good," he said briskly. "Well, I certainly have no intention of interfering, unless Kimura here gets himself arrested again, that is. One thing, though. I want to be fully consulted about any decision to publicise this as a murder investigation; and any indication of Press interest. You know what the Foreign Ministry are like when there's a foreigner involved." They did, and both nodded. "Thank you, gentlemen. I'm off to Himeji shortly. I have to give a talk at a meeting of the Housewives' Road Safety Association, and I shall make up my attendance at the Rotary Club there first. See you tomorrow, perhaps."

They all stood up, and Kimura bounded to the door, Noguchi lumbering in his wake. Otani settled at his desk to look through the day's incoming papers. He had a few ideas himself.

Chapter 4

Now peep, boe peep

KIMURA LAY BACK IN BED ADMIRING THE DELIGHT-fully formed breasts of Ulla as she pulled on a pair of flesh-coloured bikini briefs. He particularly liked the way they swayed gently as she turned to the dressing table and picked up a scrap of ribbon with which she tied back her tawny-blonde hair. Then she crossed to the built-in cupboard in her small neat bedroom and Kimura gaped in incredulity as she carefully inserted herself into a cavernous white arrangement of straps, buckles and elastic. Quite often Ulla didn't bother with a bra at all, and when she did it was in Kimura's experience a wispy fragment of transparent nylon.

"What on earth is that thing?" He was so agitated that he sat bolt upright in bed to observe her more carefully.

"It's a jogging bra," Ulla replied in a matter-of-fact way, patting her now stoutly armoured bosom and straightening one of the broad shoulder straps. She then rummaged again in the cupboard and pulled on the lower half of a blue track suit with two black stripes up each outside leg. "Just I got it, the day before yesterday. Much more comfortable, but they seems to be sold in a very high price." She pulled on the top half of the suit and zipped it up decisively. Kimura saw that there was not the slightest prospect of persuading her to get back into bed and sank back philosophically.

He enjoyed talking to Ulla in English, having convinced himself that his command of the language was much better than hers. She knew more colloquialisms, but her up-and-down intonation and distinctly Scandinavian vowel sounds contrasted, he thought, unfavourably with his own, carefully modelled on those of the cinematic superstars Robert Redford and Paul Newman. Kimura had taken the death of Steve McQueen very hard.

Ulla was twenty-seven and contrived to be both healthily interested in and distinctly unromantic about sex. She now grinned broadly at Kimura, then padded over and, perched on the edge of the bed, reached with unerring aim under the duvet and grabbed at his erection disrespectfully. "Don't look so sad, Jiro," she said, accompanying her words with a hearty squeeze which made him wince. "Save it up for Barbara tonight."

It always amazed Kimura that Ulla seemed not to be in the smallest degree put out by the knowledge of his liaison with the American, and he sometimes felt obscurely and quite illogically slighted by her nonchalance. "I'm not seeing her tonight," he replied with a touch of haughtiness. "In fact I'm not sure that I shall be seeing her again at all."

A comical grimace flitted across the fresh Nordic features. "Ha! You are perhaps frightened? Or getting short of breath? You should come jogging with us."

"Who is 'us'? Since when have you been playing *marason*?"

Ulla removed her hand, bounced to her feet and took a pair of thick woollen socks from a drawer at the side of the cupboard. Her voice was slightly muffled by the opened door as she hopped on one leg at a time to pull them on. "You Japanese are so funny to call it marathon," she said scornfully. "Jogging is quite different. It's not for hundred prozent athletes. Quite many business people, people like me. If you must know, I belong to the Kobe Club Deep Breathers and Darts Group." Kimura groaned as he tried to fathom the significance of the name. There seemed little point in working away at the advanced English conversation cassette tape course he had bought at Maruzen's bookshop if his confidence could be so undermined by this girl's easy familiarity with current slang and what he suspected to be an in-joke. If a Swede could fit in so naturally to the Anglo-American environment of the Kobe Club, why couldn't a Japanese? "Also, you don't 'play' jogging. You jog. I jog, you jog, he she or it jogs."

"You're wrong," Kimura objected. "*I* don't jog. *I* stay here and take a bath. How long will you be?" It was six forty-five by the small battery clock on the bedside table, and Kimura was not due on duty until nine. He seldom stayed overnight at Ulla's flat, but enjoyed it enormously when he did. His own apartment, though small, was comfortable enough and the women he took there often commented with some surprise on the fact that he kept it looking so pleasant. Ulla's place however, like those of many women living happily alone, had a gentleness about it which lingered in the air, or more likely the flowers which he could never bother with himself.

"About three quarters of an hour," Ulla said, glancing at the clock herself. "Please make my coffee ready at seven-thirty." She wagged a stern finger at Kimura, and was gone. Left to himself, he took a leisurely bath, and shaved with a throwaway plastic razor from the packet of several which he had presented to Ulla some time before and which were kept in the bathroom cabinet. Using ordinary soap was a little inconvenient, and he made a mental note to provide a tube of brushless shaving cream for use on future occasions. Although anxious to disengage himself from Barbara, he looked forward to a long and pleasant association with Ulla, who would with any luck be living in Kobe for at least another year or so before being transferred away from Japan.

He kept an eye on the time as he dressed and ground the coffee beans in the electric mill with special thoroughness before putting a filter paper in the Melitta funnel and pouring the just-off-the-boil water carefully over the aromatic powder. It was a lovely morning, and even though the kitchen of the third floor flat had little natural lighting, the sun streamed in when he opened the curtains of the small living-room. Kimura had turned on the radio and was listening to the country and western records played by a strenuously friendly disc jockey on the Far East Network of American Forces' Network when he heard Ulla's key in the lock and she came in, pink and almost indecently vigorous. She was breathing heavily, but looked so perfectly content that Kimura was briefly tempted to look into the idea of taking up jogging himself. The vision of himself in a smart Adidas tracksuit quickly faded, however, and he went into the little kitchen and poured out a mug of black coffee for Ulla, who accepted it gratefully from the sofa on which she had flopped.

Kimura turned off the radio and sat backwards in an upright chair, his arms folded on its back and his legs stretched out on each side. He looked at Ulla with genuine affection. "Well?"

The clear grey eyes looked back over the rim of the coffee mug. "Well what?"

"I mean, did you have a good run?"

Ulla nodded. "Terrific. Almost hardly anybody about. Japanese people get up late in the morning, that's for sure. Never do I see a shop open before about ten."

Kimura was on the defensive. "Maybe, but think how many you see open till nine or ten *at night*. That didn't happen in Europe when I was there. See any of your friends?"

"A few. Some of us meet at the same time every morning at the Kobe Club and jog round the backside in a big circle. About four kilometres. With several people one is less tempted to cut short the run. Tokyo joggers are lucky. Once started the circuit around the Imperial Palace moat you are more or less must finish."

"Tell me about them." Kimura was curious to hear more about the group of foreigners who undertook this daily mortification.

Ulla put her empty coffee mug down, stood up and crossed to the bedroom. Through the open door Kimura watched her strip off her clothes. "Later," she said. "Shower first." It was no more than five minutes later that she emerged from the bathroom, tying the simple cotton belt of her blue and white *yukata* round her waist. Kimura followed her into the kitchen and watched her make toast in the small electric grill. "Let's see," she said as she set the timer dial for four minutes. "There were today six of us. Duane Kowalski from the American Consulate General—Lindy didn't come—Geoff Withers from the Hongkong and Shanghai Bank, and Alison Jenkins with him. She is fat, but more because from eating of the baby pills. And of course the Carradines."

"You mean the British couple with the Rolls-Royce? Why 'of course'?" Kimura's face betrayed nothing of his surprise at hearing of Angela and Patrick Carradine in this connection. In any case, Ulla was busy taking butter and strawberry jam out of the refrigerator, her face turned away.

"Listen to the famous detective," she said. "And saying, I don't think I'll let you come to bed with me again until you show me your dossier on me."

She turned her head and put her tongue out at Kimura, who had coloured very slightly. He would have liked to deny the very idea of having Ulla's name on a police file. "My so-called dossier on you," he announced stiffly, "consists of a photocopy of your Ministry of Foreign Affairs identity card—which I notice you did not take with you as you should have done when you went for your run—and a note of your address and telephone number. The police keep a record of foreign residents for their protection, as you know perfectly well."

Ulla winked conspiratorially. "How do you know the Carradines have a Rolls-Royce then? What else do you know regarding to them? Not as much as I do, I'll bet." Her remark puzzled Kimura, but he passed it over.

"You said 'of course the Carradines'," he persisted. "Are they specially keen on jogging?"

The bell on the electric grill sounded, and Ulla took her toast out. "Fanatics," she said tersely. "They never miss a morning, even after . . ." Her voice died away unexpectedly.

"After what?"

"Nothing. Stop acting like a policemans and asking questions." Ulla took a huge bite at the toast which she had now spread thickly with butter and jam, glancing at her wrist-watch as she did so. "Good heavens, look at the time," he thought she said, though it was difficult to be sure when she talked with her mouth full. It was in any case still not yet eight, and he was not aware of there being any particular hurry.

"Sorry," he said perfunctorily. "I didn't mean to sound inquisitive about your friends. You mustn't be suspicious though. Surely you heard that an English lady was taken ill and died at their flat a few days ago? Food poisoning, I believe. Naturally a report was made to us at headquarters by the patrolman who was called out when they sent for an ambulance."

Ulla nodded, a shadow over her normally cheerful face. "Yes, I heard," she said, then licked at a spot of jam on her finger. "It must have been terrible. Poor Mrs Baldwin. Pop went her happiness, just before they were due to leave. As a matter of fact, I was supposed to go to the party, but something came up at the last minute."

A near miss indeed, and Kimura decided not to push his luck by probing Ulla's knowledge of the Carradines any further. "Yes, well. You see, I just happened to see some paperwork which mentioned Mr and Mrs Carradine as the hosts, that's all. Well, I suppose I'd better be going." For all his cosmopolitan style, Kimura was gauche and awkward about leave-taking in circumstances like these. "Er, thank you, Ulla. It was . . . very nice."

Her mouth twitched, and Ulla stepped forward and

gave him a friendly hug and a jammy kiss. "Very nice," she agreed gravely. "Give me a call soon. Okay?"

He was fully dressed except for his jacket, which he slipped into as he went towards the door. There he turned, still oddly sheepish. "Okay. Thanks again." Ulla blew him another kiss as he let himself out.

Ulla's flat was much nearer to the centre of Kobe than his own, and Kimura set out to make his way to headquarters on foot. It was true that there wasn't a great deal of activity so far as shops were concerned, except for a few tobacco kiosks and coffee bars in which quite brisk business was being done with the office workers who had their breakfast in them. Kimura often took advantage of the typical 'morning service' bargain available at his own favourite, the 'Empress'. Normally coffee cost two hundred and fifty yen, but until eleven in the morning a hard-boiled egg and two thick slices of buttered toast came with it for a mere seventy yen more.

There was plenty of traffic in the streets though, and here and there tradesmen were beginning to show signs of life. Kimura skirted an area outside the Mitsubishi Bank where the janitor was hoovering the swept pavement while chatting to the old woman from the greengrocer next door. She had already cleaned her section and was spraying water over it from a bright blue hose. Kimura took evasive action without being consciously aware of the fact, so normal were hazards of this kind before life in the city moved into top gear in the mornings.

He was in any case absorbed in reflection about Patrick Carradine. There was nothing surprising about Ulla's acquaintance with him and his wife: Kimura had been doing his present job for long enough to have learned very well how tightly-knit the expatriate business and diplomatic community was. There were of course the odd little special interest groups: the British with their rugger team, the business associations, the teachers of English and so on. Then again, those who stayed longer, like the missionaries and those who were married to Japanese, tended to live much less conspicuous and interrelated lives. What intrigued Kimura in this instance was the notion that Carradine might be involved in criminal activities on a large scale: it was hard to get used to.

Kimura had been reasonably truthful in implying to Ulla that the Hyogo police file on her and on most foreign residents in the area was very basic and seldom consulted. He and his men had a special responsibility for the security of the diplomatic missions and of their personnel, and the Ministry of Foreign Affairs supplied the necessary information about people like Ulla as a matter of routine. Kimura also had instant access to the operational duty commander of the riot police detachment who were on twenty-four hour standby in case of any kind of demonstration, and all the consuls and consuls-general knew how to summon immediate help. The only individuals Kimura bothered to find out much about in the way of background were those who had significant brushes with the law.

He had at first been incredulous when Noguchi asked him what he knew about Carradine; the incredulity springing mainly from astonishment that Noguchi had so much as heard the man's name. It was well known, but not in the circles in which Noguchi habitually moved. Patrick Carradine, aged forty-eight, was one of the leading foreign residents of Kobe, and was the head of his own small but prosperous trading-house. He was also one of a select group who had actually been born in Japan, and the record showed that apart from the war years which he had spent with his parents in Australia, he had lived for most of his life either in Yokohama or in Kobe. Over the years Hyogo Police had amassed a considerable amount of paperwork about him, but all of the most innocent kind. He was one of those model foreigners who never forgot to renew his Alien Registration Certificate at the proper time, whose accountant was scrupulous to ensure that his tax affairs were always in order, and whose expensive cars were duly taxed and insured.

Kimura always read the English-language *Mainichi Daily News* with its particular coverage of events in and around Osaka and Kobe, and noticed the Carradine name coming up in the social columns with almost monotonous regularity. The evening of the party was the first time he had consciously set eyes on Angela Carradine, and on looking through the file afterwards he found himself in warm agreement with the gossip writer who had described as 'stunning' the new Mrs Carradine on her arrival in Kobe three years before.

There was no evidence that Carradine had previously been married, although he was a good deal older than his wife. Kimura had much less information about Angela Carradine. The photocopy of her Alien Registration Card showed her to be twenty-nine and the holder of a British passport issued in London, though she had been born in a city called Norwich. They had no children, and Kimura supposed that at his age they were unlikely to embark on a family.

At Noguchi's insistence Kimura had checked with the immigration authorities both at Osaka Airport and in Tokyo and obtained a note of all the occasions in the past two years when either of the Carradines had left Japan. The list was not all that long, and not untypical in what it revealed of the movements of a well-to-do businessman and his wife. There had been one absence of five weeks with the destination given as London, three shorter trips to Hong Kong, and one to Korea. Noguchi had displayed signs of animation on hearing of the last, even though Kimura pointed out that the Carradines had gone together and that until the change of government there Korea had been a popular place for short holidays. It was after all only an hour or so by plane to Seoul, and the hotels were cheap and good. He knew, because he had been himself, and had greatly enjoyed a memorable evening in a *kisaeng* house at remarkably moderate cost.

When he reached the major crossing in front of Sannomiya Station Kimura noted the time by the huge digital display on the side of the Yamaichi Securities Building. Eight-forty. He would be in his office in five or ten minutes, and intended to look again through the Carradine file, as well as those of the members of the Madrigal Circle. It had proved more simple than Kimura had expected to obtain a full list without imperilling the confidential nature of the enquiries thus far.

The funeral of the late Dorothy Baldwin had taken place at St Michael's Anglican Church, and the newspaper had announced in the course of a brief obituary notice that the music was provided by the group of which she had been the guiding spirit. It was simplicity itself to telephone the church office in the capacity of a journalist on the staff of the *Music-Lover* magazine preparing an article about the resurgence of interest in European music of bygone centuries; though it had been Migishima rather than the virtually tone-deaf Kimura to whom the ruse occurred and who carried it through with some panache. Kimura had already known the name of the awkward Mr Hagiwara, and it seemed that the older Japanese ladies were Mrs Ebihara, the wife of a professor at the municipal University of Foreign Studies, and Mrs Ikeda who was married to a doctor, which accounted for the sumptuousness of her kimono. The girl whom Kimura remembered as having been distinctly attractive was, it seemed, called Kumiko Mochizuki, and she worked in the City Planning Office. He would have rather liked to look personally into her background, but the task of carrying out a confidential check of the Japanese members of the group of singers fell to Inspector Sakamoto's section, and Kimura knew that such was the distaste with which Sakamoto viewed him, he would be kept at a long arm's length.

In any case, he was quite looking forward to finding out more about the five foreign madrigal enthusiasts who survived Mrs Baldwin. Kimura was a tolerant man, and his interest in Westerners sprang from a consuming curiosity about foreign ways. When, as he frequently did, he came upon evidence of peccadilloes on the part of his charges he seldom did more than muse about them. Although he boasted outrageously about his understanding of Western psychology and frequently lectured Otani on the subject, the fact was that Kimura was a comparative cultural anthropologist of considerable acuity and practical experience.

He turned the corner and mounted the stone steps to the main entrance of police headquarters. Somewhat to his surprise, Migishima was in the entrance hall evidently lying in wait for him.

"Morning," he said amiably as the young man stiffened and bowed. "Looking for me?"

"Sir," Migishima began, gazing past Kimura's ear. "Sir, the Superintendent wishes to see you at once. He summoned me early this morning when he couldn't reach you by phone."

Kimura's heart sank. He made for the broad staircase,

Migishima at his side. "Have you any idea what it's about?"

"He asked to see all our notes on the Baldwin case, sir. He has been asked to call at the Ministry of Foreign Affairs Liaison Office in Osaka at ten-thirty."

Chapter 5

Doe you not know . . .

AMBASSADOR ATSUGI, THE NEW HEAD OF THE LIAISON office maintained by the Ministry of Foreign Affairs in Osaka, was a very different sort of man from his predecessor Tsunematsu. With Tsunematsu, however devious and complex the approach, and however maddening his courteous refusals to cooperate had been, Otani had always sensed a fundamental identity of attitude and a common background. Tsunematsu was a man about his own age, and must therefore have spent some at least of his formative years under the shadow of militarism and total war.

Now, although the office in which he was received for the first time by the new man looked much the same as it always had, the atmosphere was transformed. In the first place, Atsugi looked very little older than Kimura, and he was a big man who towered over Otani. Then again, he dispensed with any of the normal polite preliminaries about the weather, or the trouble Otani had been put to in making the journey to Osaka. To cap it all, Otani had a strong suspicion that the Ambassador was about to try to shake him by the hand; but he forestalled him by bowing with formal courtesy before seating himself in the easy-chair the big man indicated.

"I would have come over to Kobe," he boomed amiably. "I like the food over there, especially some of the Chinese places. Not as good as San Francisco though." Otani studied him warily. Atsugi's Japanese was somehow awkward. He dispensed with many of the polite forms, but the result was unlike the unvarnished style of Noguchi. It was a little like that of a foreigner, and indeed this large, breezy man seemed out of place in the quiet room with the glistening conference table surrounded by upright chairs each with an antimacassar on the back, and the magnificent *bonsai* tree in its great ceramic bowl on a table by one wall.

Silence was a tactic Otani frequently adopted quite deliberately, but on this occasion he was genuinely at a loss for words. The effect was nevertheless to put Ambassador Atsugi somewhat on the defensive. "I was Consul-General there for a few years. Spent most of my career in the States as a matter of fact. You know, Superintendent, when they gave me this assignment I thought I'd be able to forget about murder for a while." He beamed expansively and smacked his own thigh. "Well now, what about this English woman?"

Otani had been warned that this would be the subject of discussion, but neither he nor Kimura had been able to guess what interest the Foreign Ministry might have in the affair. The role of their liaison officer in the Kansai area was largely ceremonial. In the old days all of the consular offices of the various countries who needed them had been located in Kobe. A good many still were, but the economic importance of Osaka and increasing concentration on trade promotion work had prompted others to move to the larger city, and the Foreign Ministry had set up shop there too. Otani had been pretty sure at the time that this was as a result of political lobbying by the powerful Osaka prefectural Governor. In physical terms it meant little: the two cities formed a conurbation with a number of minor municipalities wedged between them, and from city centre to city centre took only half an hour or so on one of the several private railway systems. Nevertheless, in coming to Osaka Otani had left his own jurisdiction, and it was always mildly irritating to be brought face to face with the fact that the centre of political gravity of the area had shifted twenty miles east in his own lifetime.

"What about her?" Having complained so vigorously in the past to his colleagues and to Hanae about the unhelpfulness of Atsugi's predecessor, Otani had not intended to be so wooden when establishing himself with the new man; but he felt thoroughly ill-at-ease. Atsugi had made no attempt to present his name-card, and Otani sat twisting his own up in his palm. It was all very well to be brisk, but the Foreign Office man went too far. "I'm perfectly willing to discuss the matter if you can persuade me that it's any business of your office."

One of the younger man's luxuriant eyebrows rose, and a sharpness became apparent in the previously relaxed baritone voice. "I wouldn't have asked for this meeting if it *weren't* my business, Otani-san." Again this disconcerting informality. It jolted Otani to be addressed by his name rather than by title. He stirred uneasily in his chair, and Atsugi leaned forward.

"Let's get a few things straight, shall we? You know my job. I represent the channel through which all the consular officials in Osaka and Kobe deal with the Japanese Government. There isn't a great deal to do: most of them have their own lines to their embassies in Tokyo, who have direct access to my Ministry. You and your opposite number in this prefecture are for all practical purposes the only two police chiefs with diplomatic premises to protect outside Tokyo. I know what you're going to say: you have a lot of other things to do besides. Of course you do. All the same, once in a while our responsibilities overlap. How often did you have to deal with Tsunematsu before I took over? Once, twice a year maybe?'' Atsugi suddenly grinned. ''Didn't like him much, did you? It might surprise you to know he thought a lot of you . . . well, he did his job as he thought best, and I'm going to do mine in my own way. Superintendent Otani, you might as well get used to the fact that I aim to help you all I can.''

Otani grunted in a non-committal way, looking Atsugi straight in the eye. ''I mean it,'' the diplomat insisted. ''And as a demonstration of good faith I'd like to make it clear that the decision whether or not to publicise this business as a murder investigation is entirely up to you.''

Otani bristled, and only with considerable difficulty managed to keep his voice level. ''Very kind of you, Ambassador. However, I had never supposed otherwise.'' The very idea that the former head of the office had left patronising comments about him on some file or other outraged him. When Tsunematsu had been transferred under a cloud to an African republic with a particularly disagreeable reputation Otani had allowed to Hanae that he felt quite sorry for him: now he wasn't so sure.

Atsugi heaved a showy sigh. ''Look, I'm sorry Superintendent. I've been out of Japan for a good many years. I've lost the trick of your kind of diplomacy.

Let's try it another way, shall we? Why don't you ask me what I know about all this, and why we're involved?"

It seemed one way out of the impasse, and Otani nodded, his indignation subsiding. "Very well. What leads you to suppose that there may be anything suspicious about the death of the English lady? Then again, she was a housewife, married to a businessman. Nothing to do with the Consular Corps—so why your concern?"

The atmosphere lightened, and Otani began to entertain a flicker of hope that he might come to like the new man once he became accustomed to his un-Japanese style. Atsugi leaned back and flung one leg over the other. He was wearing heavy American-looking shoes with moulded rubber soles, and several inches of hairy leg were revealed above his very short, bright scarlet socks. "Right," he said with satisfaction. "I'll start the other way round, if you don't mind. And in order to do that I have to tell you some of the other aspects of my job. Of course, I know you have occasional briefings from the security liaison staff with the National Police Agency, and you're aware of course of the two main organisations of Koreans living in Japan. The bigger of the two has links with the Pyongyang communist regime in the north, and the other one reports to the KCIA in Seoul. At least they used to, before the KCIA kidnapped Kim Dae Jung from that hotel in Tokyo and smuggled him back to Seoul. And we all know what happened after that."

Otani nodded. He and his men had some anxious moments during the aftermath of the Kim show trial. The Korean community in Kobe was one of the largest in Japan and was for once virtually united in its support for Kim. The demonstrations had been ugly but it had proved possible to contain them and to keep them away from the Korean Consulate General in Ikuta Ward. Atsugi continued, his manner now more restrained. "Colleagues of mine at the Ministry have the job of thinking out policy towards South Korea for the future, but there's also been a lot of anxiety in the Justice Ministry about the realignment of pressure groups of Koreans in this country. In confidence, I have to inform you that I'm a member of an interministerial team set up to report on such trends as we can discover."

Atsugi fell silent, and gazed steadily at Otani for several long seconds before seeming to make up his mind to go on. "We have some undercover help, of course."

It was Otani's turn to take some time to choose his words. "I would suppose you have," he said at last, cautiously. The relationship between the police and the shadowy security agency whose existence was never formally admitted by the Japanese authorities was a sore point with Otani, whose own police career had begun in the immediate postwar period. At the time of the surrender he had been a very young and junior officer in the Intelligence Department of the Imperial Japanese Navy, and in a matter of weeks he had been summoned for interview by a screening board set up to choose key people for the new civil police force.

Otani remembered the experience vividly, not least because his father had in a final show of parental authority forbidden him to obey the summons. Professor Otani had been one of the few scholars of eminence to make no secret of his hostility to the wartime regime of Tojo and the militarists, nor of his contempt for the police forces with their arrogant teams of 'dangerous thoughts' interrogators. Otani had believed at the time that there was a real chance of a radical change of course for Japan. His father was impervious to his arguments, and it was many years before the old man could bring himself so much as to refer to his only son's profession, let alone grudgingly concede that the postwar police had something to be said for them. The interview, in a bare room which felt cold even in the warmth of the Tokyo autumn, as though warning of the bitterness of a bleak winter ahead, took a long time, even though only one of the four men on the opposite side of the table actually spoke to him. He was a fair-haired young American in naval officer's uniform, who spoke Japanese like a native. An older man, an Army major, sat next to him, and they sometimes conferred briefly in an undertone. Then there had been two civilians, a Westerner with a cold, hard face beneath his crew-cut, and one Japanese, silent but watchful and in the formal dress of a senior official, though his black jacket was crumpled and threadbare, and Otani could see that the stiff wing collar was several sizes too big for the shirt, being held only tenuously in place by the broad black-and-white striped tie.

"Is that all you have to say?"

The question was mildly put, but it brought Otani back to the Osaka of the affluent eighties with a jerk, and he glanced apologetically at Atsugi. "I'm sorry. I was remembering something," he said. Then the words tumbled out. "Let me tell *you* something, Ambassador," he began. "My first job was in Intelligence, years ago when you were . . . Probably just beginning primary school. I was in the first group of officers recruited to the police after the war. In those days, and right up till the Occupation ended, we did our own political undercover work. I don't say the Americans kept us in the picture completely, that would be unreasonable. But I can tell you this—there was better collaboration between us and their security people than there seems to be nowadays." It was extremely unusual for Otani to talk about himself, but there was something about Atsugi that encouraged him to continue. "You obviously know that I didn't get on so well with Ambassador Tsunematsu. The main reason was that on a number of occasions he interfered with my work. I don't call that collaboration; not when your side are playing various games of your own at the same time and deliberately keeping us in the dark."

"Yes, yes, you're right to be irritated. I'd be the first to agree that the briefing arrangements are inadequate."

This time Otani did not even attempt to suppress the snort of indignation the diplomat's remark deserved. "Inadequate? They're a joke. Every few months I'm summoned with all the other prefectural chiefs to Tokyo. We sit in rows in a lecture hall like a crowd of students and listen to some jumped-up young man solemnly telling us a lot of things we've all read in the newspapers anyway. I don't know where your people recruit your so-called 'researchers'. If the National Police Agency sent me a young assistant inspector of that sort of quality I'd send him back on the next train, I can assure you. Why, my drugs section chief has forgotten more about the Koreans living around Kobe than you'll ever learn."

Otani sat back, feeling oddly refreshed by his outburst. He had experienced anger in that conference room on previous occasions when confronting the bland, silver-haired Tsunematsu, and had, he thought, spoken his mind more than once. It was different this time, though. He seemed to be getting through to Atsugi, who nodded thoughtfully. "Your Inspector Noguchi is certainly famous in his way. And he knows the Koreans. He should do, having them in the family."

Otani became very still. When he spoke, his voice was level and quiet. "Inspector Noguchi was born in

Aomori Prefecture. Both his parents were Japanese. The family has deep roots in that area. He served with distinction in the war, and is nearing the end of a unique police career. What are you implying?"

Atsugi delved into the pocket of his jacket and produced a crumpled piece of paper which he straightened out and consulted. "Not a question of implying, Superintendent. Didn't you know that until she died five years ago Noguchi lived with a Korean woman as his common-law wife? And that he had a son by her?" For a moment Otani thought he would try to face the man down. Even among a race of people schooled to conceal their emotions Otani was renowned for his poker face, but this was too much for him.

"I didn't know," he said flatly. "I never . . . enquired into his private life, and he has never spoken about it."

"No offence, then, Superintendent. You could have come by the information easily enough if you'd had a mind to." It was true. Otani knew that he was unusual in taking little interest in his colleagues as private persons. He could hardly avoid hearing about at least some of Kimura's adventures, but had never been near any of the numerous flats he had occupied over the years. He had attended a number of funerals involving visits to the homes of police officers in his time, but it came as no surprise that Noguchi had allowed no word to slip out about the death of the woman who had shared his life for . . . how long?

"Tell me. About the woman. And the son." It was hardest of all to visualise Noguchi as a father, but Otani had no inclination to doubt the authenticity of Atsugi's information.

"They were together for over twenty years," Atsugi said quietly. "She never changed her name, and the boy took hers. Lim. Of course the Chinese character they use to write it is the same as for our 'Hayashi'. He uses whichever reading suits his purpose at the time. Mrs Lim, his mother, ran a small grocery shop and always paid her taxes for it in her own name. Noguchi lived there, of course, and my information is that he wanted to marry her. The neighbours say how attached they were. But she never would. Thought it would hamper his career, I suppose."

Atsugi paused to give Otani the opportunity to comment, but he sat quietly, his thoughts spinning round in confusion. What Atsugi said was true. Otani shared many of the prejudices common among Japanese. With part of his mind, the part nourished so tirelessly by his father throughout his boyhood and puberty in the Sino-Japanese and Pacific wars, he acknowledged the injustice and cruelty of the blank and continuing refusal to admit Japan's minorities to full citizenship and esteem, and he felt an emptiness at the thought that through no fault of his own he had spoken no word of comfort to his old friend and colleague at the time of his bereavement. Yet all the while another image jarred at his consciousness. He remembered the time before her marriage when their daughter Akiko had formed a transient attachment to a Chinese boy, a student from Taiwan, and heard himself railing at Hanae, ordering her peremptorily to put a stop to it. The idea of marrying outside one's own kind was deeply shocking to him, and he knew in his heart how superficial was his inheritance of his father's liberalism in such matters.

"I'll go on," Atsugi said after a while. "The boy was bright, and he did well at the Korean primary and middle schools in Kobe. If he'd stuck to the name Hayashi and taken a different direction, well, we might not be sitting here today. But he became a committed activist, and took himself off to high school in Tokyo. Then to the university they run for their own people there. They take their line from Pyongyang, as you probably know. Sorry. That's a very roundabout introduction, but now I can bring you up to date . . ."

Chapter 6

Away with these selfe loving lads . . .

KIMURA LOOKED AGAIN AT THE LIST IN FRONT OF him, wondering where to begin. Ten members of the Kobe Madrigal Circle had been present at the party, though the full roster supplied by the church numbered fourteen, including the late foundress, Mrs Baldwin. It had not proved to be too difficult to find out which four to eliminate, since two non-Japanese members belonged to the consular corps and Kimura knew them by sight. He was confident that neither of them had been there on the evening of Mrs Baldwin's death. Inspector Sakamoto's team had been able to advise about the remaining two: a member of the staff of the huge Sumitomo trading company on temporary assignment to Kuala Lumpur, and the principal of a girls' junior high school who was recuperating from a hysterectomy.

It was only on rare occasions like this that Kimura entertained a flicker of envy over the ease with which the criminal investigation section could cast an eye over any Japanese with even the most tenuously settled way of life. All they had to do was send a man along to the appropriate local police box and have a word with the senior patrolman whose responsibility it was not only to maintain a complete register of local residents but to visit each household at least twice a year for a bit of a chat. In most city blocks there was a fishmonger, a greengrocer-cum-general store or a tobacconist; usually all three, and what the patrolman didn't know about the details of life in the little community the shopkeepers or the postman certainly did. The fact that Japanese postal addresses have an internal logic incomprehensible to anyone outside the immediate neighbourhood leads to virtually lifelong assignment of postmen to particular routes, and they could if they had a mind to it deduce all manner of interesting conclusions from the pattern of correspondence of any one of their charges.

This convenient network of intelligence sources broke down miserably in the case of foreigners. Kimura knew he was in a minority in enjoying their society; a recent national poll had confirmed it by revealing that over sixty per cent of the population wanted nothing whatever to do with non-Japanese. This was not to say that those respectable foreigners resident in Tokyo, Yokohama, the Osaka-Kobe area and a few other major cities were actually denied the services of the postman or the support of the police when required; but merely that local Japanese interest in their activities was virtually nil. Then again, they seldom if ever patronised local shopkeepers, preferring to have their groceries delivered by the Meidi-ya supermarket which made fat profits from the huge mark-ups they justified by specialising in imported goods and employing people to write the display signs in English. Kimura had to look into the backgrounds of the *gaijin* on his list by different methods. The very word *gaijin*—outsider—emphasised the specialist nature of his skills.

Of the men who had sung during Mrs Baldwin's demise the eccentric and incompetent Mr Hagiwara was Sakamoto's concern. Kimura greatly preferred investigating foreign women, but decided to defer that pleasure until he had first dealt with the three men on his list. The little man with the surprisingly booming voice must be Frederick Austin, aged forty-four, departmental manager of the old British firm that seemed to have a finger in everything from Scotch whisky imports to container shipping. The young man with the beard had to be Donald D. Schaeffer, in possession of a cultural visa to study the economic history of Japan with reference to trading patterns in the nineteenth century with a view to completing a doctorate at Columbia University: while the old fellow with the blue eyes was undoubtedly René Laurent, the former French consul who had settled down in retirement in Kobe. None of these seemed to be a likely candidate for the role of Mrs Baldwin's murderer, but then Kimura was still at a loss for ideas in the matter of motive. The lady had certainly struck him as being imperious and somewhat disagreeable, but hardly to the point of making anyone homicidal, except possibly her husband George, who was as a matter of course in principle the prime suspect. He had been on the other side of the room throughout the relevant period, however, and although it was not inconceivable that he might have had an accomplice, Kimura felt no inclination to follow up the wild theories offered by Otani at their conference. He would of course have to check up on the obvious things like insurance policies, but if indeed George Baldwin had planned to do away with his wife he had certainly decided upon an unusually complicated and hazardous method by which to proceed.

Kimura also seriously doubted whether it was worth bothering with old Laurent. Although he had not recognised him by sight, he knew of his reputation as unofficial leader of the French community and constant source of irritation to the incumbent French Consul General. M. Laurent was active in good works, being on the board of the Catholic mission hospital, the international school and several charities. Kimura knew that he had a Japanese wife who never appeared in public, and had been amused when told that Laurent occasionally hinted that his own father had been the fruit of a liaison between a French Minister and a Japanese geisha, like the famous Satow brothers fathered by the British Ambassador, a copy of whose book on Diplomatic practice reposed unopened on a shelf in Kimura's locker.

Mr Austin would be difficult to approach except head-on, though Kimura briefly toyed with the idea of passing himself off as a newspaper reporter, as he had done more than once in his career. On the whole, he concluded, it would be safest to begin with the young would-be Dr Schaeffer, who as the holder of a cultural visa was almost inevitably in technical breach of Japanese law. Kimura referred to the separate sheet of paper in his folder on which the details about Donald Davenport Schaeffer were summarised. He was twenty-eight years old, a native of Indianapolis, and had graduated from Indiana State University. Notwithstanding this unpromising start in life he had obviously done the right thing in moving to New York to take a master's degree in Asian Studies at Columbia University, which Kimura knew to be in the senior American academic league. Schaeffer's sponsor in Japan was a professor of Kyoto University of whom even low-brow Kimura had heard, having seen him on various television programmes, though not so frequently as the ubiquitous Professor Adachi who lived downstairs from the Carradines. At all events, Kimura entertained no doubt whatever that Schaeffer was picking up some money by teaching English somewhere or other. All the young men did, not having other obvious possibilities open to them as in the case of the girls.

Kimura picked up the telephone and rang the number given as that of Schaeffer's lodgings. It was eleven in the morning and he had no expectation of finding the American at home. In fact, it was a matter of satisfaction to him that the phone was answered by a Japanese woman whom from her voice Kimura judged to be getting on in years. It was child's play for Kimura to assume the role of a casual acquaintance of Schaeffer's and elicit all he wanted to know from her. Schaeffer-san was teaching at the Elite English Conversation College in Nishinomiya, and was not expected back before evening.

The sky had clouded over during the past hour or two, and when he reached the entrance hall and looked outside Kimura almost turned back to fetch an umbrella but then decided to risk it. It seemed that the Elite English Conversation College was very near the national railway station, and he could easily take a taxi if it came on to rain. Indeed, the girl in the office of the college had laid stress on the convenience of its location from the point of view of public transport when Kimura telephoned, and had clearly hoped that he might be a potential client. Kimura was waiting until he saw her before deciding whether to sustain her in this belief.

Japan National Railways charge quite a lot more for the ride between Osaka and Kobe than either the Hanshin or the Hankyu private systems which also offer cleaner and more comfortable trains, and it had been some time since Kimura had used the cavernous national station at Sannomiya. At least he had room to stretch himself in the nearly deserted train, and almost dozed off for a while during the twenty-minute run to Nishinomiya.

He emerged from the exit the young woman on the phone had recommended, and looked around. The clouds had piled up even more than before, and had taken on a purplish tinge which looked ominous, so Kimura was glad that a large sign in clear view announced that the Elite English Conversation College was hard by. He approached the shabby building. It seemed that the language school occupied the two upper floors, since the ground floor was given over to a cheap bookstore devoted to paperback fiction and magazines, and those nearly all comics, with such names as 'Erotopia' and 'Hot Dog'. Interested though he was in sex, Kimura found them distasteful, but was fascinated and delighted to see Schaeffer of all people browsing furtively among them.

With the briefest sense of regret at the realisation that he would not now have the opportunity to meet the college secretary who had sounded so appealing on the phone, Kimura moved towards Schaeffer's side and himself picked up and leafed through one of the highly-coloured periodicals on display. He said nothing, but his proximity clearly made the young man uneasy, especially as Kimura half-turned towards him and peered over his shoulder. The glossy magazine Schaeffer was studying was harmless enough, as such things went. Two well-endowed blonde girls were depicted in unconvincingly lesbian poses beside a swimming pool, their bikini bottoms firmly in place in deference to the Japanese censors' sensitivity about pubic hair.

The American looked up, and Kimura caught his eye and nodded amiably at him. Schaeffer coloured, hurriedly replaced the magazine and made his way out of the shop, Kimura following. This disconcerted Schaeffer even more, and he stepped out briskly towards the station. Kimura let him buy his ticket and go up the stairs to the platform before following suit. There were very few people in the station, and Kimura glanced at the timetable display and noted that the next rapid service train was not due for another twelve minutes. Schaeffer had not noticed him, having seated himself in one of the bright blue plastic seats at the far end of the platform. By the look in his eye when he looked up and saw Kimura taking the next seat to him, Kimura judged he had Schaeffer nicely off balance. He spoke to him in curt Japanese. "Excuse me. I am a police officer. May I please see your Alien Registration Card?"

The American must have understood, because he sagged visibly and Kimura heard him mutter "Oh, Jeezus." Kimura helpfully pulled out his own identification folder and tried to flip it open as he had seen it done so many times on TV; but the plastic was stiff and he had to open it out with both hands to display his photograph.

Schaeffer scarcely glanced at it, but made no move to reach into his own pocket. "I am very sorry," he said in correct but heavily accented Japanese. "I don't have it with me at the moment."

Gratification suffused Kimura's being. "You are aware that you are required by law to carry it on your person at all times?" The young man scowled sullenly as he nodded his head with reluctance. Continuing in Japanese, Kimura took a small notebook from his pocket. "What is your name?"

"Schaeffer. Donald Schaeffer."

"Nationality?"

"United States."

Kimura noted that instead of using the word *Amerikajin* Schaeffer specified *Beikokujin*, a much less common usage. Although he knew perfectly well what the man's name was, Kimura made him spell it out and wrote laboriously in his notebook as he did so. "Where were you intending to go now?"

"I'm going to Kobe. I have business there."

The loudspeaker above their heads crackled into life, and a recorded voice announced that the rapid service train to Sannomiya, Kobe, Akashi and Himeji was approaching. Kimura nodded slowly. "Correction," he snapped. "We're going to Sannomiya. We have business at police headquarters." The train pulled in and they both stood. For a moment Kimura thought that Schaeffer might against all common sense make a bolt for freedom, but after a long hesitation he boarded the train as the departure bell shrilled, Kimura close behind.

After a protracted silence during which Kimura tried to assume the kind of ramrod bureaucratic woodenness which he knew would have come so naturally to his colleague Inspector Sakamoto, Schaeffer began to plead with him, pointing out that he could produce his identification immediately if permitted to go to his lodgings. Then he stressed the importance of his appointment in Kobe city. Finally his manner changed to one of weak belligerence, and as the train slowed down on approaching the Sannomiya complex which is in practice the hub of communications for Kobe city, much more important than Kobe Station itself, Schaeffer was blustering ineffectively, warning Kimura that he would be complaining in the strongest terms to the American Consulate General.

Kimura let him run on in Japanese, interjecting only an occasional "Is that so?" or "You should have thought of that before" to keep him going while he studied Schaeffer's face. Kimura thought the big brown beard ridiculous, although Schaeffer seemed to prune it now and then, in that the effect was not too unkempt. Nothing of his chin was visible, but the mouth looked as though he kept it habitually pursed when not in use.

As Schaeffer's petulant monologue ran on, Kimura was visited with the odd notion that the luxuriance of his beard had had the effect of drawing all the nourishment from his scalp, since the hair of his head was not only paler in colour but wispy and insufficient. His eyes were a lustrous brown, though, and Kimura saw intelligence in them as Schaeffer wrestled to put together sentences which, considering his agitation, emerged as quite creditable Japanese apart from the horrible American twang.

Schaeffer fell silent as the train stopped and Kimura rose, then sighed audibly before resigning himself to the inevitable and accompanying him. It had begun to rain: no more than a few spots, but they both looked up at the sky which was now completely grey. "Police headquarters, did you say?"

The fight seemed to have gone out of Schaeffer, and his tone was subdued. Kimura nodded. "Yes. Only a few minutes on foot, and part of the way we can keep under cover." They set forth, and Kimura couldn't resist another thrust. "By the time you're allowed to leave again, the rain will certainly have finished. If not, there are plenty of cheap umbrella shops round here."

Kimura could not guess at this stage whether Schaeffer had taken him for a senior officer or simply a plainclothes patrolman. He was entirely confident that it would never occur to the young man to recognise him as the deferential waiter at the party, and led the way to the main entrance of Hyogo Prefectural Police Headquarters. He was gratified to notice out of the corner of his eye an even more dejected slumping of the shoulders as Schaeffer registered the promptitude with which the uniformed patrolman on duty in the lobby leapt to his feet and gave Kimura a smart salute, which Kimura acknowledged with an affable nod. He knew the men called him 'Heart-throb' and other names behind his back, but was on good terms with most of them.

It was not until he was ensconced behind his desk in the small office he had to himself on the ground floor and had waved his captive to the upright wooden chair facing him that Kimura dealt his most telling blow to the American's esteem by switching to his excellent, easy English. "Well now, Mister Donald Davenport Schaeffer. Precisely what did you have it in mind to complain about to the American Consul General? I've met him a few times. We get along just fine. I don't believe he'd approve of your going around without your card on you. Nor of your contract with the Elite College. How much tax do you pay, Mr Schaeffer?"

Schaeffer looked completely stunned. "You speak English." The words emerged in a kind of squawk.

Kimura nodded benignly. "And you speak Japanese. Pretty good, too. Can you eat raw fish, Mr Schaeffer?" Kimura knew that this particular question infuriated foreigners resident in Japan: Barbara had told him so, pointing out with bitter emphasis that she didn't throw up her hands in extravagant but admiring disbelief every time she saw him eating a roll and butter or a plate of spaghetti. After a short but pregnant pause Kimura decided that he had softened up the American to a point beyond what was really necessary, and took pity on him.

"Relax, Mr Schaeffer," he said in a matter-of-fact way. "I guess it was a little mean of me to put you through it on the way here. All the same, your attitude left a good deal to be desired. Some of my colleagues would be tempted to throw the book at you. I could, you know. By the way, my name's Kimura. Inspector Jiro Kimura."

He extended a hand across the desk, and Schaeffer took it gingerly. His palm was soft and clammy, and Kimura surreptitiously felt for a paper handkerchief after a perfunctory handshake. As so often happened in Kimura's experience, the foreigner took refuge in a triviality when faced with a situation beyond his control. "How did you know my middle name?', he demanded intensely, as though a great deal hinged on the reply.

"What you maybe don't realise," Kimura extemporised fluently, "is that we carry out routine checks on all the language schools in the area at intervals to confirm the visa status of the foreigners they employ to teach English. Other languages, too," he added with an air of wishing to be fair-minded. "French, Spanish, German, Chinese . . . you name it. Mostly English, though. OK?" He pointed accusingly at Schaeffer. "Always catch a few. I came over there today specially to interview an American called Schaeffer. Alien registration records didn't say anything about an employment permit. So I didn't know you were Schaeffer when I saw you sneaking a look at the girlie pictures, but I already knew what his middle name was."

Schaeffer had again gone crimson with embarrassment, when an afterthought occurred to Kimura. "You wouldn't want your students to see you with that kind of material would you? Conspicuous person like you. You ought to do that kind of thing some place else you know."

When he spoke again, Schaeffer's voice was low. "What are you going to do?"

"Nothing much," said Kimura cheerfully. "They tell me you're a good teacher."

It was a shot in the dark, but it scored a bull's-eye. Schaeffer raised his head and a smug expression settled on what was visible of his features. "I *am* good," he confirmed. "Very good."

"Is that right?" Kimura was all scholarly attention. The interview was shaping up nicely. "What else are you very good at, Mr Schaeffer? Your visa application says you're researching Japanese economic history. What else do you do, when you're not studying or teaching or getting a buzz from dirty pictures?"

The reminder that he was in an extremely vulnerable position was not lost on Schaeffer, who subsided again. Kimura leaned forward and lowered his voice. "Any other hobbies, Mr Schaeffer? Are you perhaps helping Japanese economics along a little by pushing drugs? I'm looking for a *gaijin* who answers your description. He was seen in the company of a well known hoodlum, let's see now . . ." Kimura continued to decorate his fantasy with convincing detail as he pretended to consult his notebook and finally mentioned three dates and times. "Can you account for your movements on those occasions?" he demanded in the manner of Perry Mason.

Flustered, Schaeffer fumbled for a pocket diary and asked for the dates and times again. Then relief came. He looked up. "Yes, I can," he said firmly. "Once I was teaching a class, and both the other two times I was singing."

"*Singing?*" Kimura managed to fill his voice with incredulity.

"Yes," Schaeffer confirmed loftily. "Singing. As a member of a very fine specialised choir. The Kobe Madrigal Circle."

"And what in the world is a Madrigal Circle?" enquired Kimura innocently. It had taken a little time and trouble, but it would be plain sailing from then on. Being one himself, he was quite good at dealing with conceited persons.

Chapter 7

Down in a valley

"DO YOU REMEMBER," OTANI BEGAN CAREfully, "back in the late sixties, when you were, um . . ."

"Throwing Molotov cocktails in your direction and getting teargassed for my pains," responded his son-in-law, nodding helpfully.

"Yes, well, I wasn't particularly thinking of that aspect," Otani said.

Now that Akira Shimizu was a section head in the trading company for which he had worked for a good many years and was in line for accelerated promotion to department head, it had been quite simple for him to agree to meet his father-in-law for the quiet talk over lunch which had been urgently and unexpectedly sought. Not only was he under no pressure to account for his movements, but he commanded a considerable expense account about which Otani frequently twitted him.

The two men were sitting in the Leach Bar of the Royal Hotel in Osaka, conveniently near Shimizu's office, and a good place for conversation. Named for the potter Bernard Leach whose work is regarded with reverent awe in Japan, the bar houses a number of examples of his work, carefully and artfully displayed. It was the first time for Otani to visit this particular hotel, which he ruefully noted was in a price bracket he was unlikely to aspire to, and he modestly nursed a small glass of beer in spite of Shimizu's genial suggestion that he should try something a little more exotic.

He now surveyed his son-in-law reflectively. Shimizu's transmogrification from radical extremist student militant leader to exceptionally promising middle manager in one of the bastions of Japanese capitalism was interesting rather than astounding. Quite a few of the young men who had achieved prominence in the bewildering proliferation of factions of the All-Japan Federation of Student Associations during the heady days of Mao's cultural revolution in China, the barricades and pitched battles in Paris and the student rebellions in so many other countries, were now comfortably ensconced in salaried jobs in Japanese business; though it was true that comparatively few had done as well as Shimizu, whom Otani had first met on the occasion of his arresting him on the campus of Kobe University.

In those days Otani had been an Inspector, in charge of the divisional headquarters covering the university area; and his job had not been made simpler by the fact that his daughter Akiko was a student there, and gave her allegiance to the particular variant of Maoism professed by Shimizu's faction. When Shimizu had been released after questioning, Akiko Otani was one of the most strident of the group of supporters waiting outside her father's headquarters in slogan-daubed T-shirts, waving banners inscribed in blood-red with annoucements of total war against the system. Even at the time, and bone-weary as he was, Otani had wrily noted the preponderance of girls thronging round the good-looking fanatic, but would have dismissed as pure fantasy the notion that within a surprisingly few years the young man would become one of his valued friends and confidants.

"I was thinking more of the ideologies. The connections, I mean. You had international links, of course, but you spent so much time fighting it out with the other factions that I wonder how you managed them."

Shimizu raised an eyebrow. In his mid-thirties he was still lean, and there was an authority about him which commanded attention. Sitting there in his dark business suit, white shirt and discreet tie, he looked a man to be reckoned with: just as he had always seemed to Otani. "Suppose you tell me what's on your mind," he suggested.

Otani nodded without seeming to notice himself do so. "I've just come from a rather worrying meeting," he said, then took a quick swallow from his beer glass. "I can't go into full detail. At least, not yet. But I need your advice about politics. Especially in connection with Korea. Did your people have any contacts there?"

Shimizu's face clouded. He was normally much less embarrassed than Akiko to be reminded of his past activities, and reminisced cheerfully enough when sitting at ease over a flask or two of *sake* in the Otanis' house about the sometimes violent confrontations between his followers and the police, but showed little disposition to talk politics. "You mean the north, of course. Things change, you know. You're talking about fifteen years ago. Yes, there were messages of solidarity and so forth, but all the factions tended to exchange them. You could hardly expect people in North Korea, China or the PLO for that matter to understand our internal quarrels.'' He smiled briefly. ''I'm not absolutely sure I understood them myself.''

''What about contacts with the Korean political groups here in Japan? Surely you must have had local arrangements to coordinate your various demonstrations.''

Shimizu looked at his watch. ''We ought to go and eat,'' he said. ''The Prunier Room here has good fish. It's all right, I'm not trying to avoid your question, but it would be easier if I knew why you were asking it.''

Otani pursed his lips and shook his head unhappily. ''I'm sorry,'' he said. ''All I can tell you is that I'm interested to know whether you knew any of their activists personally.''

Shimizu rubbed his nose. ''Well, I certainly met some. It was a strange situation. We were on the same side, theoretically, but they hated us as Japanese. The colonial oppressors of former times. They couldn't see that kind of thing was over and done with.''

''Is it?'' Otani's interjection was gentle, but it stopped Shimizu in his tracks.

After leaving the Foreign Ministry office and making his impulsive telephone call to Shimizu, Otani had walked to the Royal Hotel by a roundabout route along the canals which once earned Osaka a description as 'the Venice of Japan'. By the late twentieth century it could only be applied with the heaviest irony, now that the canals were lined with office blocks and the sunshine rarely reached the surface of the water beneath the expressways built on massive stilts to snake their way through the only available spaces. Even so, in early autumn the black, polluted water smelt less offensive than in summer, and once in a while a barge puttered its quiet way like an old blind mole searching for the still busy harbour in Osaka Bay.

Otani was by temperament and a lifetime's habit a thoughtful man, but rarely troubled himself with broad issues of principle. He brooded over problems which actually confronted him, but took little interest in the social and political questions which were debated in the endless round-table television discussions. During the riots and occupations of university buildings of the sixties he had done his duty as he saw it, and when Shimizu ranted and screamed his 'demands' the implications of the young man's political views scarcely occurred to Otani. The new knowledge that his old comrade had a half-Korean son burned in his mind, though, and for the first time in his life Otani consciously addressed himself during his stroll to pondering the unenviable situation of the Korean community in Japan.

"Do you really think the Koreans here think the days of exploitation are over?"

Shimizu gaped at Otani in astonishment, then leaned back in his chair and blew a long exhalation from distended cheeks. "I never expected to see the day when you'd say something like that," he said at last.

Otani made a gesture of irritation. "Never mind that. Let's just say that I'm not surprised to hear that your Korean allies didn't care much for your company. Can you remember any names of those you had dealings with?"

Shimizu was still seemingly stupefied by his father-in-law's apparent sympathy with Korean aspirations, and Otani repeated the question rather sharply. "Names?"

Shimizu pulled himself together and whistled soundlessly as he pondered. "They all seem to be called Kim or Chun anyway, don't they?" he said after a while. "There was definitely at least one of each."

Otani could hold back no longer. "Lim. What about Lim, or Lin? That's another common Korean name."

Prompted thus, Shimizu nodded slowly. "Yes, of course. There *was* a Lim involved, from that Korean university in Tokyo. At least, that's what the others called him. But when I first met him he used a Japanese name . . . I can't recall what it was."

"It was Hayashi, of course," Otani snapped. "Same name, Japanese reading of the character. I always thought you were an educated man, Akira-kun."

Shimizu blinked under the assault, as unexpected as the previous radical sentiments. "Yes, it *was* Hayashi," he conceded. "Now let's go and eat. I'll try to remember as much as I can if you'll just stop bullying me for a minute . . . I can't imagine what's come over you.

Otani smiled suddenly, and drained the last of his beer. "Sorry," he said. "It *was* a long time ago, as you say. Take your time. I want to know as much about Hayashi as you can tell me. I had a feeling you might have come across him." They both stood up and Shimizu led the way to the Prunier Room, where he was greeted as a familiar and valued patron by the head waiter.

That evening at home, Otani mentioned to Hanae that he had met Shimizu for lunch at the Osaka Royal Hotel, but when she pressed him for details was quite unable to recall what they had eaten. Later still, as he lounged in his favourite spot leaning against the doorway while she washed the dishes, Hanae wondered aloud whether he could remember what they had just had for supper. Otani merely made a vague gesture with one hand and played safe by assuring her that it had been delicious.

He was indeed enmeshed in a confusion of thoughts and emotions, and the ordinary routine of home-coming had scarcely impinged on his consciousness. He was wearing his blue and white cotton yukata with the broad silk sash, and must therefore have had his bath in the usual way. "Did you wash my back for me this evening?"

He spoke more abruptly than he had intended, and Hanae glanced over her shoulder at him in some surprise. "Yes. Surely you can remember that. Though as a matter of fact I think you'd be sitting there still if I hadn't come and hurried you along." Hanae was not greatly disturbed by Otani's distractedness. It was somewhat out of the ordinary but she had seen him switch off from normal communication often enough during their years together to realise that there was little she could do about it.

"Why don't you go and see if there's anything you like on the TV?" she suggested, and Otani grunted and drifted into the allpurpose downstairs living-room. Once there, he settled himself on one of the flat cushions on the *tatami* matting and picked up the remote control box which he normally enjoyed playing with; but then pushed it aside again and lay flat on his back with his head cradled in his hands reflecting once more on what he had learned during the day.

Shimizu had tried to be helpful, but without knowing the precise reasons for his interrogation he inevitably roamed down a number of irrelevant sidetracks in the course of casting his mind back to the various conferences he attended in the sixties as one of the leading student activists in the Kansai area of Japan. Lying at ease on the *tatami*, Otani unconsciously smiled as it occurred to him that now, fifteen years later, he was in possession of information which the specialist investigators of the National Police Agency would have given their right arms to have had at the time.

It would have been too much to hope that Shimizu had been on intimate terms with Lim/Hayashi; and it seemed that he had met him on no more than three or four occasions, which were however memorable for the acerbity of their exchanges. Shimizu and those other Japanese student leaders in roughly the same camp found themselves in ideological agreement with the Korean students, but there had been bitter disagreement over tactics. Otani now knew why the group of Japanese who hijacked an aircraft and forced the pilot to land in Pyongyang were still, many years later, living under conditions of ostracism and semi-imprisonment in North Korea, and was shocked to think that this son-in-law might conceivably have been one of them, had negotiations taken a slightly different turn.

He knew also that Noguchi's son was physically totally unlike his father, being thin and wiry. Although extreme in his views and intense in his manner, he seemed however to have inherited some of Noguchi's capacity for detachment, since Shimizu recalled that the man he thought of as Hayashi kept a conspicuously cool head, given the volatile and excitable state of mind of all the conspirators.

Shimizu knew what had become of a few of his own comrades from these days, and Otani laughed out loud when his son-in-law confided that he and two or three others regularly met for an annual reunion dinner at one of the better restaurants in Tokyo. Shimizu knew nothing of Hayashi's subsequent career, however, and with his new-found sensitivity Otani conceived the notion that even the formerly idealistic man who had married his daughter and given Hanae and him a grandson had no taste for the society of Koreans.

Otani was in several minds about what to do next. It was possible, indeed probable, that the National Police Agency had a file on Hayashi. He would certainly have been under surveillance at some stage, but any surviving record would be of little present use, even though as a prefectural commander Otani could have discreet access to it if he cared. In view of what Atsugi of the Foreign Ministry had said it was abundantly clear that their own shadowy 'researchers' had long since taken over from the police, and Otani entertained no hope of being permitted by Atsugi to form his own opinions after seeing what material he and his so-called committee had at their disposal. Atsugi would be the filter through which any information would pass from the security authorities.

In the latter part of their conversation Atsugi told Otani that Hayashi was known to have made during the past ten years at least two trips to North Korea, both of them clandestine. There might well have been others. The Marine Self-Defence Force maintained patrols in the Japan Sea, but anybody could get to the off-shore islands without formality, and there were fishermen with well-equipped vessels quite capable of making the tricky but perfectly feasible voyage to the North Korean approaches without much likelihood of being spotted. As a former officer of the Imperial Navy Otani found it difficult to get his tongue round the phrase 'Marine Self-Defence Force', but he knew quite well that what Atsugi said was true. One of the more intriguing developments in post-war organised crime was the way in which the gangsters had forged links with fishing cooperatives operating from the north of Hokkaido and along the Japan Sea coast and its off-shore islands. For all their loudly-proclaimed right-wing protestations of patriotism and devotion to the Imperial ideal, the gang bosses were severely pragmatic when it came to smuggling and barter deals.

Their agents on the fishing boats dealt impartially with the Russians and North Koreans on the one hand and South Koreans and Taiwanese on the other, making enormous profits from bartering electronic and indeed all kinds of Japanese consumer goods from clothing and ball-point pens upward for gold in the north and drugs in the south. The traffic in people was much less extensive, but it certainly went on.

Otani had not thought to ask the direct question, and now found himself wondering whether or not Hayashi was thought to be currently in Japan. And like a persistent, discordant accompaniment, the connection with Noguchi nagged at Otani's mind. Recollections of innumerable conferences in his office swirled in his mind into a single image; of himself sipping green tea and going off at tangents, of Kimura examining his nails or fussily adjusting his trouser-crease, and above all of Noguchi, mountainous and immobile, contributing only the occasional unvarnished comment or suggestion. Otani found it hard to credit that for much of that time the man who gave the impression of immunity from ordinary human concerns must have been occupied with worries about a son who could in the nature of things have no straightforward life ahead of him, about the woman who shared his life but would not marry him, and with pain over the loss of them both.

Otani opened his eyes slowly as he felt Hanae's lips on his forehead. She looked down at him in silence from the kneeling position she had quietly adopted, then slid down to one side of him, supporting herself on one elbow as she kissed him again, this time on the lips. They could both remember a time when this was considered to be a shockingly lewd action, and even now it was something that happened rarely between them. Hanae's lips were soft and warm, and Otani closed his eyes again for what seemed a long time, until the gentle mouth was raised and came close to his ear. She needed to do no more than murmur. ''Shall we go to bed?''

Chapter 8

I care not for these ladies

"THE IMPORTANT THING," KIMURA EXPLAINED loftily to Migishima as they approached the house, "is to realise that the foreigners in Japan are basically very insecure. Even if they speak some Japanese they realise that they can never fit in. And when they have to cope with officials, they get very anxious." Migishima nodded, saving his breath. Like many of the more expensive houses in Kobe, that of the Byers-Pinkertons was situated on the precipitous slopes at the northern limits of the city, though surprisingly close to the central shopping and business areas. It was another pleasant day, and Kimura had unilaterally decided that they would walk to their destination. He was still slightly jealous of Ulla's jogging exploits.

"Have you got the map?" Again Migishima nodded, and produced the folded paper from his pocket to consult as Kimura continued to stride on briskly. It was one of a collection which had been amassed by the members of Kimura's section over the years of their dealings with foreigners, who customarily have them printed to distribute to their invited guests. In setting up their appointment with Mrs Byers-Pinkerton Kimura had as was quite usual inquired about the exact whereabouts of the house, which turned out to have been formerly occupied by a member of the Consular Corps.

It had not taken Migishima long to rummage through the collection and find the appropriate sketch plan. "Turn left at the *sake* shop and then it's the third house on the right, nearly opposite a kindergarten," he concluded.

Both officers were in plain clothes. In deference to Mrs Byers-Pinkerton's British nationality, Kimura had selected one of the more conservative suits in his collection, a neat grey pin-stripe with which he was wearing a plain white shirt and a dull green silk Christian Dior tie. He had hesitated over the choice, deciding in the end against a club stripe largely on the grounds that Superintendent Otani's modest range of neckwear rather surprisingly included one of that kind. Kimura felt obscurely put out whenever his chief appeared sporting it. Migishima, of whom at one time Kimura had virtually despaired, was arrayed in a light sports jacket of perfectly satisfactory cut, and if his shoes still reflected the taste of the former patrolman on the beat, his trousers were at least of fashionable length.

The street with the *sake* shop on the corner was quiet at that hour of the afternoon. The kindergarten children had long since gone home, and the small playground in front of the single-storey building was deserted save for an old man moodily sweeping the cracked concrete with a long broom made of twigs bound round a bamboo shaft. An amateurishly lettered poster announced the kindergarten's Sports Day for the following Saturday and promised grilled squid, chicken kebabs and many other delights for neighbourhood residents who turned out to cheer the children on.

This British family were not diffident about making the whereabouts of their home known to all and sundry. On the plaster wall at the corner beside the *sake* dealer's sign was a wooden plaque with one end tapered in symbolic arrow form. It was painted white, and in bold black letters bore the name BYERS—PINKERTON. Kimura pointed it out to Migishima. "There we are," he said. "That way." Such signs indicating the way to foreigners' houses are commonplace in Tokyo, Kobe and other large cities with sizeable expatriate communities, and Kimura had long ceased to find them in any way remarkable. Indeed it amused him that they irritated Otani so much, provoking him to short-lived explosions of displeasure whenever they came across one together. It was quite useless for Kimura to explain that foreigners actually liked people to know where they lived, unlike Japanese who preferred such information to be restricted to members of the family and a very few others with a legitimate need to know.

The names of all householders in Japan are required by law to be displayed outside the premises they occupy, but this was a very different matter, Otani argued, from putting up vulgar signs at a distance, like those used to lure customers to bars and sauna baths. Certainly the sign outside the Byers-Pinkertons' front gate was larger and bolder than the discreetly carved wooden name-plates of their neighbours, who were, Kimura noted in passing, the Shinomuras, with the Wakasugis next door. "Baiaazu-Pinkaton," Migishima read aloud from the phonetic Japanese script under the English names. "Funny how some of the most complicated foreign words go fairly easily into Japanese sounds."

Kimura sniffed. "Hardly complicated," he said, pressing the button on the Ansafone device at one side of the solid metal gates. "Not as foreign names go, that is."

The box emitted a crackle and a squawk. The person speaking was obviously Japanese, and Kimura announced his name and affiliation in response. A moment later there was a buzz and a click from the gate, which Migishima opened to admit them to a most un-Japanese front garden. In the first place, the pine and plum trees and stand of bamboo which grace all Japanese gardens on account of their propitious nature were absent, even though the plot occupied by the house was much more spacious than usual. There was a tree, a handsome maple whose delicate small leaves were just beginning to hint at the fiery glory to come in November. There were rose bushes still opulently in flower, and most amazing of all at that time of the year, an expanse of smoothly mown grass of rich emerald, quite unlike the grizzled brown tangle found here and there in public open spaces.

The house itself was, Kimura thought, probably prewar. The architectural style was ponderous but comfortable, and had it not been for the television aerial and the solar hot-water panel mounted on the roof's southern aspect, he could have imagined himself in another age in another culture. Migishima was in any case in a condition of awed silence, and they approached the heavy white painted wooden front door with delicate steps. Kimura was curiously scrutinising a highly polished brass coach-lamp mounted at the side of the door when it opened, to disclose a Japanese maid.

Kimura could remember a time when most of the better-off expatriate households boasted full-time domestic staff, and it was still by no means uncommon for well-off Japanese to employ a girl from the country or even a distant relative in reduced circumstances to take care of the cleaning and laundry. The increasingly affluent sixties and seventies had however sucked most Japanese out of domestic service and into well-paid jobs in industry, commerce and the hotel and catering trades. Those foreigners well enough off to run to a domestic mostly had to look to Filipino women as potential employees, or make do with part-time help secured through agencies like the Kobe Maid Service and Baby-Sitting Agency which had so readily empanelled Kimura and Migishima some months earlier.

It was therefore all the more surprising that the person who now confronted them was like somebody out of a book or an old movie. She was elderly, perhaps in her late sixties, and both tiny and birdlike; and performed an odd bobbing movement the name of which Kimura had to look up in his Japanese-English dictionary afterwards. The English called it a curtsey. It was her uniform which astounded the two men, however. The old soul was got up in a black dress the skirt of which terminated in the region of her skinny knees, revealing stick-like legs in thick and wrinkled black stockings. Tied round her waist were the strings of a tiny starched white apron, and although inside the house she was wearing shoes. Perched on top of her sparse grey hair was a white lace cap.

Without conscious reflection, Kimura bowed at the apparition and murmured apologies for the intrusion, while Migishima looked round at the entrance hall and hastily shuffled back into the shoes he had half kicked off as with a wealth of polite imperatives the maid urged them towards an open door just as they were. It seemed extraordinary to him not to change into the backless slippers kept just inside the front door of every Japanese home.

The room into which they were ushered was spacious and had a lofty ceiling from which hung an old-fashioned chandelier. Long net curtains at the big windows muted the sunshine outside, and there was a pervasive smell of furniture polish. The floor was of glowing dark wood, mostly covered by a huge Persian carpet in which rich reds predominated, and a grand piano occupied most of one corner, sheet music scattered over its closed top. There was a fireplace with a mantelpiece over it, on which stood several photographs in silver frames. As the maid withdrew and closed the door behind her Kimura crossed the room to look at them. The largest picture was of a plump girl in a wedding dress, a blank, dazed smile on her face, and at her side a man in a morning suit with what seemed to be fair hair brushed cruelly and gleamingly flat. His unremarkable features were disfigured by a toothbrush moustache. The picture had evidently been taken in a studio, and bore the photographer's signature adorned with many a curlicue and flourish.

In smaller frames were a number of pictures of small children squinting in sunshine as they embraced dogs, brandished toys or consumed ice-creams; while at the end of the mantelpiece was another larger picture, of an elderly man nursing a pipe in one hand and squeezing with the other the shoulder of a white-haired lady with a gentle smile. Kimura peered at the inscription, which read 'All our love from Oomps and Doodah', as Migishima remained uncomfortably in the middle of the room standing first on one leg, then the other.

The museum-like peace of the room was then abruptly shattered as the door was flung open and a huge dog bounded in, made straight for Kimura and rearing up, placed one large paw on each shoulder and energetically licked his face as he staggered back helplessly. "Oh gosh," cried Sara Byers-Pinkerton as she entered in the dog's wake. "I had no idea of the time. Hullo! Get *down*, Gladstone," she added almost absent-mindedly as Kimura continued to struggle weakly. "It's all right, he only wants to be friends." Belatedly she came to the rescue, seizing the creature by his heavy studded leather collar and hauling him unceremoniously away. Both the dog and Kimura were panting. "*Sit*!", Mrs Byers-Pinkerton commanded as the dog continued to gaze in helpless infatuation at his prey. "I say, he really likes you. He doesn't like everybody, you know. *Sit*, Gladstone."

With obvious reluctance Gladstone lowered his hindquarters to the floor, then slumped despairingly at full length. His mistress glanced amiably from one to the other of the two men. "Do sit down too, both of you. Tea?" Kimura, still mopping the evidence of Gladstone's affection from his face, did not at first catch the question. "Tea?" she repeated. "I expect you could both do with a cup of tea. I know I could. Now for goodness sake sit down." Migishima gingerly perched himself on the extreme edge of one end of the large sofa covered in a flowered cretonne print, recovering himself as he almost slid off, while Kimura, his expression revealing a continuing wariness of the dog Gladstone, selected an armchair. "Mind the hairs," his hostess warned. "Oh, too late. Never mind. It's just that it's Gladstone's favourite chair." She picked up a small silver bell from an occasional table and shook it heartily. The maid must have been lying in wait outside the door, since the sound it produced was the merest tinkle, yet she materialised at once, bobbing again.

"Tea, please Emmy, there's a dear," Mrs Byers-

Pinkerton said, still in English, and the little person hastened away again. "Funny, isn't it? She's called Emmy. She really is. I think she's a perfect Emmy, don't you?" Thus appealed to, Kimura gazed back at a loss for words. The perfectly ordinary Japanese female name Emi carried no connotations for him, and in any case he was still trying to recover his equanimity while adjusting himself to his surroundings and to Mrs Byers-Pinkerton, who had bounced on to the other end of the sofa and curled her legs up under her, though not before Kimura had noted their no-nonsense sturdiness.

He knew Sara Byers-Pinkerton to be thirty-seven years old, and to be the mother of a twelve-year-old son at boarding school in England as well as of an eight-year-old daughter with her and her insurance broker husband in Kobe. He had only a faint recollection of seeing her in the Madrigal Circle line-up at the Carradines'. On that occasion she had, he thought, been wearing a long dress like most of the women there, and like the other singers had assumed a preternaturally solemn expression while performing. He was unprepared for the lunatic air of disorganised goodwill which emanated from the woman now beaming at him as she fiddled with the long double strands of expensive-looking pearls round her neck.

When standing she had kept her feet planted firmly apart, her hands on the solid hips under a cotton skirt in a bold checked design, apparently unaware of the fact that there was a button missing from the front of her plain pink blouse. Not that this had any effect on Kimura's sensitive sexual blood-pressure, since Sara Byers-Pinkerton's endowments were as meagre above as they were hearty below. Nevertheless, she exuded a certain animal vigour, and her brown eyes were bright in a mobile, *jolie-laide* face hard to recognise as belonging to the same person as the one in the wedding photograph of perhaps fifteen years before.

"Lost your tongues?" she enquired brightly as Kimura continued to stare and Migishima shifted uneasily a centimetre or two farther away from her.

Kimura shook his head quickly but visibly and pulled himself together. "I'm sorry, Mrs Byers-Pinkerton. I am being very impolite," he said, and produced one of his name-cards from his pocket. "Please allow me to introduce myself. My name is Jiro Kimura. This is my assistant, Mr Migishima." Migishima blinked in gratified surprise at hearing himself so referred to as his neighbour on the sofa turned her head and enveloped him in a warm smile.

"Frightful mouthful, isn't it? Byers-Pinkerton, I mean. Call me B-P, if you like. Like the Scouts, you know?" She swung round again to face Kimura, leaving Migishima with his lips moving slightly as he tried to comprehend what had been said to him. He had on joining Kimura's section drawn diffident attention to his knowledge of German, but Kimura was remorseless in his insistence that the young man should also work at English.

"Now you're the head one, aren't you. This is terrific. I don't think I've ever had a detective to tea before . . . I don't think you can count the time Sebastian let the head's car tyres down at the prep and the local bobby was lying in wait for us when we went on leave . . . oh, smashing, here's tea." Kimura went through a brief but painful reappraisal of his tactics in the brief respite which ensued as the door opened to admit Emmy tottering under the weight of a great silver tray laden with tea things, which Mrs B-P jumped up and took from her. The two of them bustled about and Kimura leaned back, trying to avoid Migishima's increasingly accusing eye.

All at once a plate was thrust into his hand and he realised that Emmy was offering him a goodly slab of fruit cake while Mrs B-P, her eyebrows high in interrogation, mouthed at him voicelessly. "Milk or lemon?" Kimura lip-read.

"Lemon, please," he said in an unnecessarily loud voice, and Migishima hastily followed his lead. After what seemed a lengthy interval the maid Emmy took herself off yet again, and Kimura summoned up his most formal manner to embark on the business which had brought them to the house.

"It's very kind of you to allow us to call here today, Mrs, er, Byers-Pinkerton," he began. He could not bring himself to address her by initials though had Migishima not been present he would undoubtedly have tried to charm the lady, who though not attractive to him was possibly not immune to flattery.

"Makes a very nice change, I can tell you," she replied through a mouthful of cake. "Sorry. Shouldn't talk with your mouth full, I know. But never mind, Gladstone will take care of the crumbs."

At the mention of his name, the now somnolent dog opened one sorrowful eye, then sighed heavily and went back to sleep. "I must say it was a bit of a shaker to hear that you think poor old Dotty Baldwin might have been done in."

Mrs B-P's face took on an expression of conspiratorial menace so comical that Kimura could only with difficulty stop himself grinning. There was undoubtedly something appealing about the woman. He nodded gravely. "Yes. We took the step of announcing that there are some doubts about the circumstances of Mrs

Baldwin's death only after the most serious consideration," he intoned.

"What a super sentence," said Mrs B-P. "You sound just like that chap, what was his name, PC49 or something."

Something had to be done. "Look," Kimura said urgently, "would you please not interrupt? I'm sorry, but actually I can't always follow what you say. I need to ask you some questions. Do you mind just answering them as simply as you can?" Mrs B-P nodded, eyes wide and one finger across her lips in a childish pledge of discretion. Taking a deep breath, Kimura began again. "Good. Right. Well, we've been able to do a certain amount of background research without letting anyone know of our suspicions. Let me say at once that we are satisfied that no member of the Madrigal Circle had any reason to wish any harm to Mrs Baldwin . . ."

He flung himself back in his chair in exasperation as the door opened yet again, this time followed by the appearance of a little girl in school uniform, complete with beribboned hat, who came in trailing a satchel on the floor behind her and made for the piano, ignoring all three adults in the room. Seating herself on the long bench, she opened the volume on the music stand and actually struck a few notes before her mother intervened. "Not now, Francesca my sweet. Besides, where are your manners? Can't you see we have visitors?"

The child glanced balefully from one to the other of the two men. "Good afternoon," she muttered, then, with slightly more animation, "Can I have some of that cake?"

"Oh, I suppose so," Mrs B-P replied. "This is Mr Kimura and this is Mr Matsu something."

"Migishima," he volunteered eagerly.

"Yes. They're policemen, Francesca."

Francesca licked one of her fingers before replying. "Have you come about the murder?" she then enquired. "Mum thinks it was that loony Japanese man."

Chapter 9

Dreams and Imaginations

THE STREET OF THE FORTUNE-TELLERS, LIKE THOSE TO be found in every great city in Japan, presented an almost medieval appearance even though it was situated in a central built-up area near the garishly lit entertainment quarter with its bars, restaurants, cinemas and pinball machine arcades. Although the racket from countless megaphones, muzak loudspeakers and shopkeepers bawling their wares was directly behind him, it was as though an invisible soundbaffling device dropped round Otani as he paused for a moment and looked along the narrow alley.

Normally at the end of the day he was taken home in his official car, but once in a while he took it into his head to dismiss Tomita the driver and make his way as he was then doing on foot to the station to join the mass of other commuters boarding the frequent suburban electric trains to the dormitory districts strung out along the whole distance between Kobe and Osaka. In his boyhood Rokko had been a village with its own identity, but now only a very few pre-war houses like his own remained among the new developments squeezed into every available plot of usable land.

The *ekisha* or fortune-tellers took up their positions after dark throughout the year, and for the most part Otani scarcely noticed them, but now they somehow forced their presence into his consciousness. Along a stretch of perhaps two or three hundred metres, in doorways and outside shuttered office buildings there were at least twenty tiny folding tables set up, each illuminated fitfully by a lantern of bamboo and white paper containing a single candle, and with a sign indicating the nature of the occult technique practised.

The majority bore the hexagram of broken and unbroken lines produced by the casting of the yarrow sticks needed for consultation of the I Ching, or Book of Changes; but as Otani strolled quietly along in the mild evening air he noticed several palmists' tables, a phrenologist, an old woman who seemed to have no particular speciality, and one evident lunatic whose table was festooned with crudely-drawn sketches of flying saucers.

Otani could not remember the last time he had given any conscious thought to the matter of fortune-telling, but being the reactionary he was he noted with some satisfaction that among the *ekisha* doing desultory business that night in Kobe were several old men in traditional Japanese dress, at least two wearing the old-fashioned round caps associated with their profession. Needless to say, these were the interpreters of the Book of Changes. One of them was talking earnestly to a young girl who could not have been more than seventeen or so, a senior high school pupil in her unbecoming dark blue serge skirt and sailor suit top, a bulging and battered briefcase on the pavement at her side. She listened attentively, head on one side as she unconsciously tugged at a knot of her coarse black hair, while the friend she had with her giggled nervously and fidgeted as she waited for the consultation to end.

Other fortune-tellers were dressed in perfectly ordinary and indeed sometimes quite smart western dress. One middle-aged man with flashing spectacles could almost have been a bank manager as he sat there in a neat dark blue suit brooding over the hand of an obvious gangster, a sharp-featured young tough in a tight jacket and white plastic shoes. Otani did not give him a second glance, but something brought him to a halt shortly after that.

About half-way down the alley to his left was a small Shinto shrine, occupying an area no more than five or six metres square. It was of a commonplace type, put up generations before by the local people when establishing their community, in order to propitiate and do honour to the spirits of the place. Tatty and rundown, it was like dozens of similar shrines in Kobe, spared the depredations of the developers because of its sacred status but neglected by the people except for one or two festival occasions during the year, when the bedraggled zig-zag paper talismans would be renewed, the offerings of rice from previous occasions cleared away from the tiny sanctuary no bigger than a small wardrobe, and the old flagged courtyard swept and cleaned.

Then perhaps a priest from one of the big, prosperous shrines in the city would come along and stand in front of a handful of shopkeepers and their families in his white and aquamarine robes, huge black lacquer clogs on his feet and wearing the headgear of a Court official of a thousand years past. Flat wooden baton in his hands, he would chant nasally in archaic language an invocation of the tutelary deities, pray for the prosperity of the community, collect his fee and depart.

As with all such shrines, the entrance to the confined precincts was marked off by a symbolic gate, no more than two uprights joined at the top by two cross-beams, the uppermost curving slightly upwards at the extremities. These *torii* gates are generally of wood painted in a shade of orange or vermilion, but the one before which Otani paused was of stone, and was flanked on either side by stone lanterns. Inside the little courtyard a tree had somehow survived. It was not particularly beautiful, but was given dignity by the plaited straw rope fastened round its girth, festooned with the zig-zag paper hangings which protected the spirit of the tree from evil influences.

The fortune-teller who had set up her table beside the tree was quite a young woman. She looked to Otani to be not a great deal older than his own daughter Akiko, probably in her early thirties. She was dressed fashionably, in a discreet skirt and sweater; wore a certain amount of make-up and looked altogether the very picture of a modest, attractive young housewife of the kind beloved by producers of television commercials. The whole area was far from dark and Otani could see her well enough in the general illumination all around, but was struck by the way the additional flickering light of the paper lantern on the table cast a gentle shadow over one side of her face and highlighted the other.

She had no client and her eyes met Otani's. The woman's expression was entirely neutral, and she made no attempt to beckon him or otherwise seek his custom. Otani was not a superstitious person and had never previously consulted a fortune-teller in his life, but quite without reflection he passed through the stone *torii*, approached the table and bowed slightly. The woman inclined her head in response. "Welcome," she said. "Please take a seat." She spoke quietly and in the manner of a cultivated person, using courteous language naturally, without the fluting insincerity of shopgirls or the announcers on railway stations.

Otani sat on the small folding wooden chair opposite her and remained silent, looking at her. She had remarkably compelling eyes, and he could not have said afterwards whether it was two seconds or two minutes before she spoke again. "Please show me your hands. Palms upwards." There was no sign indicating that the *ekisha* was a palmist, but it seemed to Otani somehow appropriate that she was, and he extended his hands obediently. The woman looked at them without touching for a few seconds, and Otani noticed a flicker of consternation pass over her features.

Then she took his right hand gently in her left and lowered her head to study his palm carefully for some time, before repeating the process with the other, in complete silence. Her grasp was firm and warm, and the sensation as she occasionally gently traced a line with her forefinger was distinctly agreeable. Finally she sat back and looked at Otani gravely. The spell was broken and part of Otani's mind woke up. All his professionalism then flooded into his consciousness and he suppressed a small smile as the woman began to speak.

A middle-aged man, well but not ostentatiously dressed? Obviously a member of the professional classes, and with an air of authority? Of course she would begin by suggesting that he was burdened with complex and heavy responsibilities. It argued no great diagnostic genius on her part for her to surmise that he was a married man, but without small children; and she was pretty safe in urging a man of his age to take care of his health. It was all very predictable, and although the voice was pleasant as the woman continued with what must have been a well-rehearsed patter, a sense of irritation began to invade Otani's mind as he ruefully reflected that he was wasting his money without even knowing how much he was going to have to pay.

The fortune-teller seemed to sense Otani's change of mood, since she stopped speaking for a moment and held his gaze with a new intensity. "Hold out your palms again," she said then almost peremptorily. Otani did so. "Look at them," the palmist commanded. Otani glanced without much interest at his hands as he held them out. They seemed very ordinary to him, the index and forefingers of his right hand slightly stained with nicotine although he smoked much less than he had done in former years, and occasionally managed to give up cigarettes altogether for a couple of weeks or so.

"It isn't your child," the woman said quietly. "But someone close to you. An old friend, or a business associate perhaps. You're very worried about him."

Otani raised an eyebrow. "How do you know?" he asked.

"Look at your forefinger—no, the right hand," she said pointing to it. Her own skin was smooth and white in contrast to his swarthiness. "See how it separates itself from the other when in repose." It surprised Otani to realise that what she said was true, and he hastily withdrew his hand and put it on his knee. "You feel a sense of separation," she went on, then closed her eyes. Even in the artificial light Otani could see her eyelids quiver slightly as she went on speaking.

"There is little you can do," she said. "He—I'm sure it is a man—he has his *karma* and you have yours. You fear that you must do him some harm. Not directly, but because of something else you must do." The dark intelligent eyes were again opened and Otani once more felt the sense of being locked to her gaze. "Am I not right?"

He avoided a direct answer. "What you say interests me very much," he said instead, leaning forward and replacing his hands on the table, but folded.

The woman seized them again, but this time simply held them in her own. The pressure was gentle, but to his astonishment Otani felt a distinct sexual excitement rising in himself. Her voice was still quiet, but she spoke with urgency. "You must do whatever is necessary," she insisted, then suddenly released him and sat back. The consultation was clearly at an end.

"Thank you. I am sincerely grateful," said Otani, beginning to rise to his feet. "Excuse me, it is very impolite on my part, but, er, how much . . . ?"

The woman smiled for the first time. She really was decidedly attractive. "Whatever you think appropriate," she said politely. "Perhaps two thousand yen?" This, the price of a lunch for Hanae and himself at a modest restaurant, struck Otani as being a bit steep. On the other hand he was considerably embarrassed by the idea of putting a price on the strange encounter at all. He fumbled in his wallet and found that it contained three one-thousand yen notes, took them out and laid them all on the table with a muttered apology. The fortune-teller inclined her head with dignity. "Thank you," she said. "Please be careful." She used the conventional phrase, but said the words slowly and meaningfully as Otani bowed in farewell and turned away.

Outside the shrine precinct again, he stood for a short time, lost in thought. A young man and his girlfriend went in, but ignored the fortune-teller and instead approached the sanctuary. They were both dressed in jeans, and looked like students. Otani heard the clatter as a few coins were thrown into the latticed wooden offertory box, and a cracked clanking as the girl shook the rope hanging below a small, cheap bell. Then she clapped her hands, bowed her head, clapped again and they both turned away, she almost skipping out of the enclosure as she clung to her boy friend's arm.

Otani realised with a start that the fortune-teller could still see him, and indeed was looking steadfastly at him. She smiled again briefly as she caught his eye, and he walked off in renewed embarrassment. For the remainder of the short walk to the station Otani turned over in his mind the unnerving relevance of what the woman had said to him. He scarcely speculated about the possible grounds for her apparent insight into his dilemma over Ninja Noguchi, but had been startled enough by it to ponder the emphatic advice she had given him.

Otani's conversations with Ambassador Atsugi of the Foreign Ministry and with his own son-in-law Akira Shimizu had provided a great deal of food for thought, but it had not taken him very long to come to at least one firm conclusion. This was that the likeliest lead to the man Lim or Hayashi was through Noguchi, his father. Notwithstanding the fact that Atsugi showed no inclination to make the Security Service materials available to him. Otani surmised with some confidence that he could make a certain amount of headway in investigating Hayashi with the assistance of those senior police colleagues in Tokyo who happened to be friends of his, but he could do nothing in relation to the Korean community in his own district without Noguchi's finding out about it. Noguchi's network of informants and contacts would without question see to that. In any case, Otani had not the faintest idea how to begin an approach in the Kobe area except by asking Noguchi to do it for him.

Otani's whole nature and every Japanese nerve in him shrank from a direct approach to Noguchi with all that it would entail. It was true, as Atsugi had pointed out, that he could probably have found out about his old associate's private background. If Noguchi had not seen fit over the years to divulge any information about it, however, it would be desperately wounding to his self-respect for Otani to refer to the matter. This would have been the case even without the crucial complication that there was now no doubt that Noguchi's son had at the very least committed acts of technical illegality, and might very well prove to have been guilty of very serious crimes.

The fortune-teller had urged him to do his duty, and Otani could see no way of obeying her injunction without directly involving, and certainly subjecting to enormous emotional pressures, one of the few people in his world whom he truly held in respect and affection. Otani sighed as he arrived at the station and found he had insufficient coins to buy his ticket to Rokko from the automatic machine. It would give-change for a thousand-yen note, but he had handed all his over to the fortune-teller and had only a ten-thousand note left. He decided to have a beer and a few pairs of sushi before going home. They would change his banknote for him in the sushi bar, and in any case he felt he could do with a drink.

Chapter 10

Can she excuse my wrongs?

"I THINK IT'S AN EXTRAORDINARY AND OUTRAGEOUS suggestion, Inspector,'' snapped Patrick Carradine, and Kimura sighed inwardly. His remark to Migishima about the basic insecurity of foreigners resident in Japan kept returning to haunt his recollection. First Mrs Byers-Pinkerton and now Carradine displayed not only perfect self-confidence but seemed to share a knack for directing the conversation themselves rather than answering his questions politely. Unfortunately he had at this stage no convenient psychological weapon to employ to disconcert either of them. Unlike the young man Schaeffer, these were persons of substance, whose personal administrative affairs were in meticulous order: he had taken the precaution of checking.

Kimura had been inside enough expensively appointed offices occupied by senior members of the foreign business and diplomatic community in Kobe not to be unduly intimidated by his surroundings, but even so there was no doubt that Patrick Carradine did himself well. The trading company of which he was President and Managing Director had its offices in the two top floors of one of the new skyscraper blocks not far from the Oriental Hotel.

Recalling the opulence and location of the Carradine apartment, Kimura concluded that he was a man who liked a room with a view. From the big windows of the twentieth-floor office, practically the whole sweep of Osaka Bay was visible in the clear autumn air, from Shirahama in Wakayama Prefecture far to the east to Awaji Island in the south-west. Shipping of all kinds swarmed in the busy Inland Sea lanes, and the new, man-made Portopia and Rokko islands east of Kobe port looked near enough to be within a stone's throw.

With some effort Kimura kept his gaze level and steady as he looked at the big man in the expensive leather armchair across from him. They were using English, though Carradine had greeted him in excellent Japanese and it was a moot point whether either had a better command of the other's language. "It isn't a suggestion, sir," he said quietly. "Believe me, we don't come to a conclusion like this recklessly. The autopsy on Dorothy Baldwin revealed the presence of tetradotoxin, one of the quickest-acting poisons known. There is no way she could have ingested it before coming to your party."

Carradine was silent for a few minutes, staring at Kimura intently. Kimura was perfectly certain that the Englishman was trying to place him, aware that he had seen him before. He was equally sure that the chances of Carradine's connecting him with the whitejacketed temporary waiter at the party were extremely slim. It had been Mrs Carradine who had perfunctorily greeted him and Migishima on their reporting for duty and shown them where they could change; and her husband had not been there when they had been bundled off unceremoniously by the local police patrolman. Mrs Carradine was an honourable woman: the fee due to the two of them for their services had been duly paid over to the agency a day or two later.

"We've met before," Carradine eventually said flatly.

Kimura shrugged. "Very probable," he replied. "My job brings me into contact with a good many of the foreign residents in this prefecture. However, that's by the way. I'm sorry if the facts upset you, but there is unmistakable and objective evidence that someone administered the poison to Mrs Baldwin while she was in your flat. Now we've investigated exhaustively the possibility that it could have been accidental. As I've just explained, the substance occurs naturally in *fugu* fish, which is served only in licensed restaurants and is not available for domestic purchase. The caterers who supplied the canapés for your party confirm that there is no question ever of serving *fugu* on these occasions. In any case, they aren't licensed, and as a matter of common sense it's inconceivable that just one and only one out of hundreds of canapés could have been tainted accidentally."

Kimura was getting into his stride, and settled himself back more comfortably in the big chair. "It's good of you to see me this morning, sir, and I don't want to take up your time unnecessarily. I speak very frankly to you because you are personally under no suspicion whatever. Our investigators have established that you were at no material time in Mrs Baldwin's proximity until after her collapse. We have also eliminated a number of others. The process continues. What I have come to consult you about is the question of motive. We are so far at a loss to form any hypothesis. Can you think of any reason why anyone might have wished Mrs Baldwin out of the way? Needless to say, any information you can give will be treated in the strictest confidence."

Patrick Carradine raised one hand to his mouth and pensively ran a finger to and fro across his lips. He had calmed down, and now looked quite composed. "I apologise for my earlier manner, Inspector," he said. "I stand corrected, but it's still an extraordinary suggestion, and the idea takes a bit of getting used to." He was dressed in a grey suit which Kimura judged with his expert eye to have cost at least two hundred thousand yen and wore with it a plain shirt of the palest pink and a discreetly patterned burgundy tie. Kimura could not place the cologne he wore, but became aware of a slight intensification of the fragrance. Good. Mr Carradine was perhaps not quite so sure of himself as he would like it to be supposed.

"Naturally," said Kimura with an air of concerned understanding. "The whole thing must have come as a terrible shock to you and Mrs Carradine anyway. But if you would be so kind as to think about my question? Perhaps you'd fill me in on why you were the hosts . . . I understand you're not members of the Madrigal Circle?"

Carradine shook his handsomely modelled head decisively. "Good Lord, no," he said with a quick smile. "Mantovani's more our style than Monteverdi."

"I beg your pardon?" Kimura was lost.

"Sorry." Carradine hastened to apologise. "Your English is so perfect that you make me forget my manners. No, my wife and I have no taste for that kind of music. They have their regular Wednesday rehearsals in our flat, though." He preened himself visibly. "There aren't too many with as big and comfortable a room as ours. Mind you, I always keep well away from home till they've all gone on those occasions. Actually, to answer your question, we gave the farewell party because Dorothy Baldwin was . . . well, quite a leading light in the British community. The madrigal business was her special hobby, but she was active in all kinds of charitable and social work. And I suppose, well . . ." At this point Carradine broke off and modestly averted his eyes. "Well, apart from the Consul General, I think my wife and I are probably, well, shall we say, about the most senior in the community here . . ."

Kimura nodded again, his face expressionless. "Indeed you are. In line for an OBE before long, I imagine?" Kimura took a snobbish interest in honours and awards of various kinds and had on one occasion attempted to explain to Otani the difference between a knight and a lord, desisting only when he realised that his superior's eyes had glazed over and that he was to all intents and purposes asleep. He did not rule out entirely from his daydreams the remote prospect that, following some masterly *coup* of police work, he would himself receive an honorary award from the hands of one of the European ambassadors in Japan; preferably the British who did these things with the most style.

Carradine looked at him sharply but affected to ignore Kimura's question. "Naturally we asked the Baldwins to let us know the people they wanted us to invite, and that included her madrigal friends. They always like to sing when they have the chance . . . to tell you the truth, they won't take no for an answer . . . it wasn't my idea to inflict that awful racket on my guests but perhaps other people enjoy it more than we do."

"So, you were acquainted with Mrs Baldwin as a prominent British resident, but not perhaps a particularly close friend, sir?" Kimura judged it time to insert another 'sir' to re-establish a respectful distance, hoping that Carradine would forget the barb in the remark about the OBE.

Carradine nodded gravely. "That is so. I know very little about the Baldwins' personal life." He seemed to have regretted his earlier candour, and to be weighing his words with some care.

"To answer your main question, I must make it clear that I have not the slightest idea why anyone should be ill-disposed to Dorothy Baldwin. In any case, they were on the point of leaving Japan. They showed every sign of being a perfectly . . . contented couple."

Kimura decided to deal at once with the flagrant lead to George Baldwin. "I will again speak very frankly, sir," he said in his best official style. "It will come as no surprise to you that as a matter of routine we carried out a thorough investigation into Mr Baldwin's circumstances and activities. We are as sure as it is possible to be that his wife's death has come as a tragic and totally unexpected blow to him."

It was true. After Otani had finally given formal permission for a Press announcement to be made to the effect that an investigation was being carried out into the circumstances surrounding the English woman's death, it had been Kimura's personal duty to notify George Baldwin before the local papers were informed. In the days immediately following his wife's death, Baldwin had been staying at the home of Frederick Austin the madrigal singer, and Kimura had been able to talk to them both during the course of a single visit. Awkward and difficult though it had been, this visit had satisfied Kimura that Baldwin was shattered by the news, and that Austin's reaction when told was not that of a man with anything to hide.

After Mrs Austin, whcse voice was as quiet as her

husband's was penetrating, led Baldwin out of the room, hollow-eyed and disbelieving, Austin spoke freely about the Baldwins. Kimura now knew that Baldwin led a mild and blameless life, that he had never been know to display anything but quiet affection for his pushy and conceited but fundamentally good-hearted wife, and that he had absolutely nothing to gain financially or in any other way from her death. As a consequence of these interviews Kimura had no hesitation in urging Otani to put no official obstacle in the way of George Baldwin's wish to leave Japan to take refuge with his son and daughter-in-law in New Zealand for a time until he was required to take up his new assignment with his firm: Austin thought he might well decide to retire.

"Absolutely. Please don't think for a moment that any other thought was in my mind." Carradine's immediate response was entirely appropriate, but Kimura thought he detected a detached or possibly distracted note in the smooth easy flow. He badly wanted to throw Carradine off-balance by introducing the subject of his possible Korean connections, but was under the strictest and most explicit orders from Otani to do nothing of the kind. Kimura seldom had any hesitation in doing things of which he was fairly sure the Chief would disapprove if he knew, but balked at deliberately contravening a straight instruction.

"Well, sir, any other ideas? I gather that the Baldwins were unlikely to be involved in any of the sort of activities that tend to lead to violence?"

Carradine's head snapped up. "I don't follow you, Inspector. What are you driving at?"

Kimura waved a hand airily. "The overwhelming majority of crimes of violence, apart from those committed by psychopaths, are motivated by greed, fear or sex." Kimura thought he had put it rather neatly, and leaned back in his chair before continuing. "Greed, fear or sex," he repeated. "Right." He raised a hand and began to tick off items on his extended fingers until he lost count.

"It looks as though we can rule out greed. The Baldwins lived on his salary, I understand. Mrs Baldwin had no private means, and only Mr Baldwin carries life insurance. Fear. Well, we're talking about blackmail, essentially. Mrs Baldwin doesn't seem to have been the sort of person who would go in for blackmail, would you think?"

Carradine's mouth tightened. "She was a great busybody, you know. Always prying into other people's business."

Again Kimura had the feeling that Carradine was trying to lead him. "What sort of business?" he enquired gently.

Carradine coloured slightly under the expensive-looking suntan. "Oh, there's no doubt she was simply a gossip. Loved hearing about anything—you know—well, you were mentioning sex. I wouldn't dream of suggesting that Dorothy Baldwin was personally involved in anything like that—she was pretty obviously past all that kind of thing. But she wasn't above whispering about other people." He glanced out of the window. "You never know, somebody might have been afraid Dorothy would put two and two together in that way. I mean, people do have affairs you know."

Kimura was the last person to challenge this simple truth, so he merely nodded and let Carradine go on, reflecting that neither Angela nor Patrick Carradine were to outward appearances anywhere near 'past all that kind of thing'. Indeed they both exuded an aura of exuberant animal health which could well indicate an appetite for sexual variety.

"I agree that it's hard to imagine Dorothy as a blackmailer, I don't think she had the imagination for that. All I'm saying is that somebody might have been frightened of her."

"The question is, who?" Kimura focused his bright black diamond eyes on Carradine's and reflected for the hundredth time in his career that it was the simplest thing in the world to know when a foreigner was dissembling, but curiously difficult to guess what he might in fact be thinking. Japanese were much more convincing liars, but it was easier by far for an experienced investigator to read their thoughts. Kimura was quite certain in his own mind that Carradine's efforts to suggest motives for the murder of Dorothy Baldwin were insincere, yet his line of reasoning was on the face of it quite sensible.

"You're one of the most influential members of the foreign community here, Mr Carradine," he continued after a moment. Obviously you're also a man of great discretion, but you must yourself hear a good deal of gossip about people? In strict confidence, I assure you. Can you think of anyone who might have reason to be afraid of Dorothy Baldwin's tongue?" Carradine closed his eyes briefly, and with a flicker of pleasure Kimura realised that he was avoiding his interrogatory stare.

"I presume you've interviewed all the members of the Madrigal Circle?" Carradine said after a pause.

Kimura nodded although the other man's eyes were still closed. "All those who were there that evening have been interviewed—oh except for one lady."

"Who's that?" The question could have been casual, but Kimura let it hang. Carradine shifted slightly in his chair and again looked at Kimura. "Have you spoken to Sara Byers-Pinkerton?" Kimura inclined his head, expressionless. This was becoming interesting, and he was not surprised when Carradine glanced ostentatiously at his watch.

"I'm keeping you, I'm afraid," Kimura suggested helpfully.

"I'm at your disposal, of course, Inspector." The reply came pat, but then Carradine cleared his throat. "But, actually, you know, I don't really think I can help you beyond what I've said . . . and that was probably more than I should have done."

"You've been most helpful, sir." Kimura injected a note of weary formality into his voice as he levered himself up out of the chair. Carradine rose at the same time, towering over Kimura as they moved towards the door together over the thick mushroom-coloured carpet.

Kimura paused by an abstract print in a metal frame on the wall, which was covered with raw silk of a kind which he knew cost a fortune. "I don't understand modern art," he observed truthfully, managing to sound as dull as he hoped he would. "That's really, ah, interesting, though." Then he whirled round in time to catch the remnants of Carradine's expression of condescension. "Planning any trips out of Japan in the near future, sir? I may need to bother you again." He waited till Carradine opened his mouth to reply, then went on. "You have my card, sir. I'd appreciate it if you'd let me know ahead of time if you have occasion to leave the country."

Then he nodded affably and reached for the handle of the door. "I'll let myself out," he said.

Chapter 11

Joyne hands

NINJA NOGUCHI SEEMED, AS USUAL, TO MATERIALISE from nowhere, and Kimura had trouble in concealing his surprise when he suddenly became aware that he had company. "I wish you wouldn't do that, Ninja," he said irritably. Noguchi made no reply beyond opening one eye fractionally wider. "I thought you said we were supposed to meet at the end of the fishing jetty."

"Changed my mind, didn't I?" Noguchi growled. "You look ridiculous in all that rubbish."

Kimura was used to being insulted by Noguchi and normally paid no attention, but he was moved to protest on this occasion. He stopped in his tracks, almost dropping the fishing rod he was carrying in its canvas bag. "Who was it that insisted I should go to the Morimoto angler's shop and get kitted out? Who was it who countersigned the bill? For the life of me I can't see how we're going to explain all this to the Public Safety Commission auditor if he picks it up; and now all you can say is I look ridiculous."

Noguchi's craggy features split into a repulsive grin. "Don't get excited," he said, unperturbed. "You always look ridiculous, but don't worry. Wait till you see the others." Kimura sniffed and relapsed into a dignified silence as they walked on past the shuttered warehouses which lined the pier. It was one which was in any case little used since the passing of the days of the passenger liners which used to call regularly at Kobe with their hundreds of free-spending tourists, and at six on a Sunday morning was deserted.

Before leaving his flat Kimura had indeed studied his mirrored reflection doubtfully, wondering whether he would in fact pass as a candidate member of the Buchi-Buchi Angling Club. The tweed jacket he felt to be quite right, and the proprietor of the shop had assured him that the waterproof leggings which squeaked as he walked would soon soften up with use. There did seem to be a great number of bags and sacks to festoon round himself, however, and his taxi driver had grumbled in a reasonably good-humoured way about the time it took him to get himself in and out. The real problem was the cap with its long heavy peak, which Kimura now knew was definitely a size too big, so that it shifted perceptibly when he turned his head quickly.

Noguchi scorned headgear of any kind, and though Kimura noticed that he was wearing rubber boots, he seemed to have made no other sartorial concessions, being dressed in his usual capacious and grimy trousers, a workman's shirt and a sagging once-white linen jacket which Kimura had seen many times before. He was however carrying a bulging canvas holdall supported by its strap across his barrel chest, and in one hand a fishing rod in a threadbare bag.

It was a dull morning, but holding the promise of improvement later, and as the two men rounded the last warehouse the harbour came into full view. There were at least twenty vessels riding at anchor in the roads in addition to those moored at various jetties; most of them small coasters, but among them several container ships waiting for access to the specially equipped unloading facilities and a couple of medium-sized tankers. Only two were on the move, heading slowly out towards the Inland Sea, but there was evidence of activity on board several of the others, and all in all the scene presented a lively contrast to the deadness of the pier behind them.

"You're sure they'll be there?" In spite of his bulk, Noguchi covered the ground with surprising speed, and Kimura found himself breathing heavily with the effort of keeping up with the older man.

"They'll be there." The assurance in Noguchi's voice was total; but as he spoke he came to an abrupt halt and stuck out a brawny arm to stop Kimura. "Over there," he then said quietly, and pointed to their left.

There were perhaps eight or nine men strung out along a narrow jetty about a hundred metres long, some busily preparing their gear, some already sitting apparently half-asleep, gazing at their floats as they bobbed gently on the black oily water. "Surely they never actually *catch* anything, do they?" Kimura was genuinely at a loss to imagine how any living creature could survive in the polluted harbour.

Noguchi made a curious half snorting, half chuckling sound. "They catch something all right," he said. "Not always fish though."

"Do you mean the whole club is bogus? How do they get away with it? I mean, the port authorities can't be that stupid, surely?"

Noguchi did not answer at once, but stood shading

his eyes as he peered at the men in the distance. "Not completely. Used to be quite above board, years ago. Used to get some decent fishing, even around here. Still catch a few, odds and ends. Chuck them back, mostly. Members were harmless old chaps, port office let them go on. Then, oh, five six years ago some local boys saw the point of joining. Show your membership card—same as you did—Customs checkpoint wave you through."

The point of their elaborate charade began to become clearer in Kimura's mind. It was indeed true that the Customs man at the gate where the taxi had dropped him had done no more than glance incuriously at the card which Nogushi had given him a few days earlier and which had enabled him to buy the cap embroidered with the coveted insignia of the Buchi-Buchi Angling Club, but Kimura had reflected at the time that he could in any case have passed through the checkpoint quite easily by showing his Hyogo Police identification. In that case, though, he would have had to state his business rather than merely struggle through the gate with his impedimenta while muttering a casual greeting.

"I see," Kimura announced judiciously. "Once inside the bonded area, they can go where they like."

Noguchi gazed at him with monumental patience. "Clever boy," he finally rumbled. "Had my eye on them for some time. Nice little set-up. Go out in a dinghy, crewmen off a freighter drop the stuff overnight in waterproof packets, little marker float, haul it in, into the pouches and away you go. See the three nearest us? Getting ready to do a pick-up now."

Kimura was intrigued, but also confused. "I see. I suppose it's worth detailing a few hoodlums to pose as anglers for the sake of the cover . . . but if you've got it all worked out, why don't you just pull them in with the stuff on them?"

Noguchi shook his head slowly from side to side. "Small fry. Trying to find out who's behind it." He fell silent and they both watched the three men in the distance as they made their way down a flight of stone steps to where a small boat was moored. Two of them carried fishing rods, while the third settled himself at the oars. The man in the bows untied the line from the iron mooring ring and pushed them away from the stone wall. There were a few comradely waves from their fellow anglers, and the oarsman paddled them out no more than two or three hundred metres, while his passengers baited their hooks and soon settled down in apparent tranquillity.

"Over here," Noguchi then said with a jerk of his thumb towards a small prefabricated hut on their left, and sauntered towards it. They were in clear view of the men on the jetty wall, but none of them seemed to be paying any attention to them, and in a few moments they were in effective concealment behind the hut, which was evidently used during working hours as a kind of rest room. Through the grimy window Kimura could see a battered table littered with old magazines, while there were a few folding plastic chairs round it and on a small side table a large thermos container on a tray with a number of handleless cups upended neatly round it. On one wall was a calendar advertising Nikka Whisky with the aid of a topless Japanese model with a bored expression on her face.

Kimura tried the door, and found it unlocked. "It's open," he told Noguchi unnecessarily. "Maybe there's a watchman about."

Noguchi shook his head. "Not Sundays. Might as well go in." Somewhat reluctantly Kimura followed him into the hut, where the air was indeed fusty and devoid of any feeling of recent occupation. There was a second window which gave a view of the harbour, and Noguchi went over to it, rummaging in his holdall as he did so. Producing a pair of binoculars, he adjusted them with considerable care and stared fixedly through them for some moments, then offered them to Kimura.

"To the left of the tanker, just beyond the container ship with the green and yellow funnel," he said. "The *Joon Hi*, out of Pusan."

Kimura raised the binoculars to his eyes and readjusted them fussily. "You ought to go and see an optician, Ninja," he muttered. "These things are focused at least half a kilometre out." The ship was clearly visible to the naked eye, but it took Kimura a few moments to make the lettering on the stem jump into abrupt clarity in the eyepieces. He then slowly raked the whole length of the ship, coming to the initial conclusion that none of the crew members was about, but then picked up a movement and saw a man in blue jeans and a dark sweater lounging against a tarpaulin-wrapped pile of crates, largely concealed by an open hatch cover.

Kimura became aware of the disagreeable proximity of Noguchi, whose personal freshness was never remarkable and whose holdall seemed to give off a stale odour of fish. He moved aside ostentatiously, lowering the binoculars with an air of irritation which was completely lost on Noguchi.

"Look. They're on the move," Noguchi muttered, pointing. In the most natural way imaginable the oarsman in the dinghy had begun to paddle again, moving the boat in the general direction of the Korean freighter but still a goodly distance away.

Noguchi snapped his fingers, and reached out for the binoculars, which he re-focused much more quickly than Kimura had done. After a further few seconds' scrutiny, he again handed them back to Kimura and began to delve into his holdall. "About twenty metres ahead of them," he said with satisfaction. "Little blue float. No bigger than a golf-ball." By the time Kimura had fiddled with the binoculars and brought the dinghy into focus, Noguchi had produced an expensive-looking Nikon camera with a motorised winder attachment, and had replaced the ordinary lens with a telephoto version.

"I can't see anything," Kimura complained, rubbing his eyes before traversing the surface of the water ahead of the dinghy yet again.

"I can," was all Noguchi rumbled by way of response, raising the viewfinder of the camera to his eye. The elegance of the high-precision camera looked incongruous in his beefy hands, but he focused it with great delicacy. Just then Kimura finally spotted the little blue object swaying gently a few yards in front of the boat, and grunted in satisfaction as Noguchi reached across him and gently slid the grimy window-pane open just wide enough to enable him to take photographs through the aperture.

Although impressed by Noguchi's preparations, Kimura was moved to criticism. "You'll never get sharp telephoto pictures without a tripod, Ninja. Too much hand movement." Noguchi ignored the remark, bracing himself against the side wall and putting the final touches to his focusing as the dinghy drifted quietly to the vicinity of the float. Kimura was now watching the anglers through the binoculars, and saw quite clearly what happened next.

The man in the bows of the dinghy and nearest the blue float hauled in his line as though to examine the condition of the bait on his hook, then reached behind him into his creel. Kimura distinctly saw the flash of silver as he carefully and almost casually attached what was obviously a live fish to his hook, then with a quick glance round flipped it over the side of the dinghy into the water. The creature had still enough life left to swim away, making the line stream out and the tip of the fishing rod bend.

All was then activity, the whirr and clash of the mechanism of Noguchi's camera reflecting the apparently cheery excitement of the men in the dinghy as the oarsman turned his head and the angler in the stern moved forward, the boat dipping dangerously as he did so. It was well done. A casual observer would have been very lucky to have noticed the blue float come aboard almost exactly at the same time as the 'successful' angler wound in his line and reached out for the hapless fish, or the dexterity with which two oilskin-wrapped packages were pulled in and stowed quickly inside the capacious canvas pouches.

The whole exercise took place a good two hundred metres from the Korean ship, but Kimura noticed that Noguchi took a few pictures of its stern before quickly taking another camera from his seemingly inexhaustible bag, this one with a conventional lens. With it he took a few general shots, establishing the relationship between the dinghy and the freighter.

Then at last Noguchi deigned to reply to Kimura. "We'll see if they're sharp or not," he said, for once not bothering to conceal the satisfaction in his voice. With the same unexpected delicacy he unloaded the films from both cameras after quietly closing the window. None of the men on the jetty so much as glanced in their direction, though the pseudo-catch by the angler in the dinghy had attracted some attention and there were signs of animation among the members of the Buchi-Buchi Angling Club which had not been evident earlier.

"I suppose they'll come in now?" Kimura enquired innocently.

Noguchi's scorn would have been withering if encountered by anyone else. "Be your age. They'll be out there for a couple of hours if they've got any sense. Probably got a couple more in the creel waiting to get caught. Anglers don't go out on a Sunday and pack it in as soon as they catch one."

"Perhaps you're right," Kimura conceded, dimly aware that he was very much the junior partner in the day's enterprise. "No more pick-ups today, though, I suppose?"

This time Noguchi actually smiled. "One kilo of that stuff is worth close on three hundred million yen, lad. Say the price of fifteen fancy cars. Or as much as you'll earn legit in your entire career. They probably pulled in five kilos there. Enough for one day?" He seemed to be about to go on, but closed his mouth again abruptly and stood stock still. Kimura's animal reflexes were not as sensitive, and it was not until he actually heard the handle of the door behind them turn that he too froze.

"Keep your backs turned," said the newcomer. The voice was light and almost pleasant. "Right. We'll begin with you, Fatso, on the left. Take your shooter out, slowly mind, and drop it behind you. Then you, Fancypants."

"We're not carrying shooters." It was Kimura who spoke. "We're—" he bit off the words 'police officers' just in time as he registered the almost imperceptible shake of Noguchi's massive head.

"You don't have to tell me," said the voice. "You're with Onodera's lot. Pretty soon you'll tell us all about it." Something told Kimura that Noguchi was deliberately keeping silent, and that he was doing so because his voice might be recognised.

Trying to coarsen his own habitually fastidious manner of speech, he tried to test the hypothesis. "How did you get on to us? See us arrive?"

"Shooters first. Not so much gab." The voice was no longer so pleasant.

"I told you. We're not carrying any."

"We'll soon see. Get that gear off." Again a hint of a signal from Noguchi, and Kimura began slowly to divest himself of his accoutrements. "Don't turn round. You'd better believe I've got a shooter. And I'll use it." Kimura was perfectly ready to believe it, and lowered his gear to the floor with care.

"Keep quite still, Fatso," came the voice from somewhat nearer, and Kimura actually felt the hard pressure of the gun barrel against his back as their captor dragged his possessions backwards with a neatly-shod foot. The crash of the gun in the little hut was almost deafening, and it was only after a second or two of black horror that Kimura realised not only that he had not been hit but that Noguchi had wheeled round, simultaneously knocked the gun out of the man's hand, and was now holding him effortlessly in a judo hold which Kimura knew from personal experience could be tightened to bring about unconsciousness in a few seconds, and was potentially a killer.

"Well, well," he was rumbling amiably. "It's Baby-Face. What are you doing up so early? Going to behave?" The face was conceivably babyish in repose but as Noguchi momentarily increased the pressure it became more contorted and the eyes rolled from side to side in desperation. "You're a nuisance, Baby-Face. And your boss won't be pleased with you. Now we shall have to pick up those lads of yours out there."

Contemptuously Noguchi released the man and flung him to one side so that he collapsed like a rag doll into a rickety chair, sucking in his breath with a horrible creaky whistling sound. It took him a long time even to recover the power of speech, and when he did so his language, to Noguchi's obvious gratification, was appalling.

Chapter 12

Shall I sue, shall I seek

"AND VERY NEARLY KILLED ME IN THE PROCESS," Kimura concluded bitterly, giving vent to his sense of grievance for the third time that morning.

Otani nodded solemnly, his face perfectly composed. "It would have been a great loss to us all, Kimura-kun," he said in a funereal way. "As I mentioned earlier." It would have been impossible to accuse him of frivolity, and the momentary twitch at one corner of his mouth could have been caused by any accidental muscular spasm, but Kimura read the signs and subsided, though with an air of offended self-righteousness.

Noguchi looked from one to the other of them, but said nothing. Never a loquacious man, he had uttered scarcely a word since entering the room a few minutes after Kimura and coming to rest in his usual chair. Unusually for these days, Otani was in uniform. The order had gone out within the last day or two for the switch to winter blues in accordance with the inexorable demands of the calendar, though the weather was quite warm enough still to have justified the coolness of the grey summer lightweights. The temperature in the room was pleasant enough, though, and Otani looked composed and efficient in the buttoned tunic jacket with its gold insignia of rank.

"Let's just say that I think the incident as you've described it was handled with commendable skill. No more than I would expect, needless to say." Otani gestured towards the glossy photographs scattered on the surface of the coffee table between them. "I don't think we shall have any trouble in persuading the prosecutor to move on the basis of this splendid evidence—let alone any statement the man . . . Baby-Face . . . what's his real name?"

Noguchi opened his mouth at last. "He's got several. We arrested and charged him as Ito. Masao Ito. It'll do for the time being."

Kimura had got over his sulks and leaned forward eagerly, all sweet reason. "The problem, chief, is that it might be much more useful in the long run to let him go. We think there's a strong chance that none of the men on the jetty realised either that he'd spotted us, or that we . . ." Even Kimura hesitated, then began again. "That Ninja managed to turn the tables. Though when I think of the risk he took—" Again he bit off the words as he caught Otani's bland eye. He cleared his throat. "Anyway, be that as it may, we both feel pretty sure that although there were undoubtedly other villains from the Miyada gang there, they would have been concentrating on making sure the pick-up went off without trouble. Baby-Face is one of Miyada's particular trusties, and was probably just nosing around with no particular business except to be around when the ones in the dinghy came ashore. He took it for granted that we were snoopers from the Onodera gang in Osaka, after all."

Otani looked at Noguchi, who nodded slightly. "I see that Ninja agrees. And you tell me that you got this man—Ito, Baby-Face, whatever he's called—you got him out through the back, out of sight of the jetty? What about the man at the gate? The Customs guard?"

This time Noguchi smiled his rare and blood-curdling smile. "I persuaded Baby-Face to come out like a good boy. Gave a little wave to the gatekeeper, he did. Three pals from the Buchi-Buchi Club." Otani did not enquire further along that line, judging that on the whole he would prefer not to go into Noguchi's techniques of persuasion.

Kimura took up the tale again. "Ninja reckoned we had time to bring Baby-Face here and still get back in time to pick up the characters with the goods. All the same, I stayed in sight of the gate, just in case."

"I hope you had your bleeper with you, Kimura-kun." Otani's voice was all gentle concern. "I wouldn't like to think of you arresting three *yakuza* carrying a fortune in snow-powder single handed."

"Oh, it was quite all right," Kimura reassured him hastily. "Ninja was back in plenty of time. He brought Migishima with him," he added as an afterthought. "Though why Migishima was hanging about headquarters at that hour on a Sunday morning I've no idea."

"Waiting for his missus," said Noguchi glumly.

"I'm not really interested in Migishima's domestic arrangements, gentlemen," Otani objected sharply, and looked at his watch. "Time's getting on and I have an appointment with the Governor later this morning. Suffice it to say that the men were, as you already reported, duly arrested with the contraband in their possession.

All this happened yesterday. So far, so good." His eyes snapped round and fixed on Noguchi, who stirred and sat up a little straighter. "You don't seriously ask me to believe that Miyada and those behind *him* don't know by now that their men are in trouble?"

"Sure they know. We saw the car waiting for them. Driver, plus one spare hand. Might have tried to interfere, too, except we had our own just round the corner. Quite a little party it was. They sheered off, but it was a Miyada car. They know about the snow all right. Not about Baby-Face though. Don't think so." Noguchi sank back apparently exhausted by the effort of speech, and Otani turned an inquisitorial eye on Kimura, who liked nothing better than to expound a theory.

"Our point is this, chief. The Miyada gang is of course affiliated indirectly to the Yamamoto network: all the gangs here are. But you know from your own dealings with him in the past that old Yamamoto professes at least to set his face against drugs. Of course he knows perfectly well what Miyada's group are into, and as long as they hand over their regular contributions Yamamoto's central organisation lets them be. Nevertheless, we're convinced, Ninja and I, that Miyada's controller is somebody else. Ninja's got a man keeping as much of a tail as possible on Miyada, but we think that if we turn Baby-Face loose we might get another chance of flushing out Mr Big."

Otani rubbed his nose dubiously. "And you really think that Mr Big as you call him is this foreigner Carradine?"

"We do, sir," said Kimura with formal dignity. "That, you will recall, is why I infiltrated his household in the first place. On a tipoff from one of Ninja's Korean canaries."

Otani glanced quickly at Noguchi, who remained impassive. Since becoming aware of Noguchi's background, Otani had found himself being more careful about the way he referred to Koreans in conversation. "Yes, I'm aware of that," he said to Kimura. "It seemed a very long shot to me at the time, and even though you've made surprising progress, there's still only a mess of unrelated circumstantial pointers that I can see."

Otani stood up, straightened his tunic and strolled over to the open window. After staring out for a few seconds he turned to face them and spoke again from where he stood. "Let me put it this way. For whatever the reason, the two of you have pulled off a splendid drugs bust, and I congratulate you. You, however, Kimura are also supposed to be investigating a murder, and we seem to be no further on that. You tell me you think there's a link. That link—*the only link* which seems to rest on objective facts, is that the murder took place in the home of a man who, on the unsupported tip of a Korean informer, is thought by the pair of you to be at the top of a huge drugs ring. This man is a solid and respected foreign resident, one of a handful. There are seventy thousand Koreans in this prefecture. I must have more than this from you. You must see that." Otani's voice held an almost pleading note. "I've read the reports on all the interviews with the members of this choir. Inspector Sakamoto's section have covered all the Japanese members quite thoroughly. Oh, by the way, he's decided he will take Migishima's wife into the Criminal Investigation Section after all. It seems she did so well with some of the interviews that he changed his mind." Otani snapped his fingers irritably. "We spend altogether too much time talking about that couple. What I mean to say was that there seems to be one left out of the foreign group your people are supposed to be handling. *Kowarusuki* or some such name. Why?''

Kimura would have liked to concentrate on the question of Carradine, but wrenched his mind back to the Madrigal Circle with an effort. ''Yes. I should have explained sooner. Mrs Kowalski. Lindy. Actually her name is Belinda. There's a problem there. She has diplomatic status: her husband is one of the economic staff at the American Consulate General and she would have to agree to cooperate quite voluntarily.''

''You've done that sort of thing before. I'm quite agreeable that you should go through the procedures. I gather you're quite satisfied that none of the others is under suspicion.'' Otani moved to his desk and absent-mindedly picked up one of the papers on it.

''That's so,'' Kimura replied. ''I saw them all myself, except for the old Frenchman. I gave young Nodo that job—his French is probably as good as mine.''

''Is that so?'' The conventional phrase emerged fruitily from Noguchi, but Kimura decided to ignore him.

''Well, if you say so, sir. I admit I'd just as soon put it off for a day or two . . .''

''Loose ends, Kimura. That's our trouble in this office, if you ask me. Until you cross her off, I shall go to bed every night convinced she's the murderer.''

Kimura nodded submissively. He had been truthful but not entirely frank with Otani. His delaying tactics in respect of Lindy Kowalski were due only in part to her diplomatic status, which did present technical but by no means insuperable problems. They were also the consequence of her membership of the jogging club, which had prompted Kimura to decide to approach the American woman in a roundabout way through Ulla. Ulla being no fool would need to be taken into his confidence, however, and Kimura had been hesitating before taking such a step. It now occurred to him that in the light of Otani's unexpected insistence on an interview it might after all be better to play it straight and go through official channels.

"There's another thing," Otani said reflectively. "I was curious about the fact that the child implied that her mother suspected a Japanese member of the choir, and said he was insane. Who could that be? Sakamoto's reports say nothing about any such person."

Kimura blinked in confusion, then his face cleared. "Oh, that! Nothing of consequence, chief. I'm afraid Migishima expressed himself badly in writing up the report in Japanese. I should have picked up the false emphasis . . . the little girl actually used the English word *loony*. A childish expression, meaning odd or eccentric rather than insane. Hagiwara is certainly rather peculiar in his appearance and manner, but perfectly sane. As you see from Sakamoto's report."

"But why should her mother have said such a thing? The child surely didn't invent it?"

Kimura shook his head knowingly. "I don't doubt that she said it, sir. Purely in a joking way, I'm certain. I was interested enough to go through Inspector Sakamoto's report on Hagiwara myself, and I discussed it with the Inspector."

"You must have enjoyed that." It was Noguchi again, and the remark made Otani smile briefly as he recalled the numerous occasions on which Inspector Sakamoto had stood before him ramrod straight but almost visibly quivering with outrage as he registered yet another complaint about Kimura's methods.

"Hagiwara is comfortably off," Kimura went on doggedly. "He is associated with the family kimono rental business, but mainly occupies himself with his hobbies, so far as anybody knows. Unmarried, which is a bit unusual for a man of his age—"

"So are you, Kimura-kun," Otani cut in. "I've offered to find you a nice girl many times. Go on."

Kimura heaved an ostentatious sigh before doing so with formal brevity. "Involvements are mainly musical. Belongs to an amateur Noh acting group in which he plays the bamboo flute. Eccentric only to the extent that he can afford to indulge his enthusiasms."

Otani nodded. "Very well. We must accept that none of these people—barring the woman you haven't seen yet—seem to have had any rational motive for murdering the English woman, and you don't think Hagiwara is unbalanced to the point of doing it irrationally. That brings us back to Carradine. If your theory is tenable, he would obviously go to some lengths to protect himself. But I insist that you've produced nothing significant to back up the original tip-off."

"We have now." Noguchi spoke with flat authority, and Otani looked at him with interest.

"Oh? What?"

"The *Joon Hi*. The freighter."

"What about it?"

Kimura intervened in the staccato exchange with enthusiasm. "That's what we've been trying to tell you, Chief," he said, springing up from his chair and flinging his arms out dramatically. "Carradine's firm includes a small shipping agency department, and they're handling this particular ship. In fact they're almost exclusively concerned with freight to and from Korea, mainly Pusan."

Otani sat down slowly and carefully at his desk, leaving Kimura alone on his feet in an attitude of triumph. The three men presented a curious tableau. Noguchi had produced a matchstick with which he was picking such of his teeth as remained to him, while Otani was toying with his treasured paper-knife, the one fashioned in the shape of a miniature samurai sword, complete with purple silk tassels. Kimura held his pose for a few moments, and then dropped his hands slightly self-consciously and put them behind his back in the manner of the Duke of Edinburgh, whom he occasionally took as one of his more mature Western models.

"I see," Otani said at last.

"Found out this morning," Noguchi rumbled, peering at his matchstick with an air of disappointment.

"Yes. Well, that certainly puts a new complexion on things. Interesting. Very interesting." More possible titles flashed across his mind unbidden: 'Deadly Cargo', perhaps, or 'The Poisoner from Pusan'. He pulled himself together. "So you both think that this man Ito might help to reinforce the link? Do sit down, Kimura." Kimura had begun to pace back and forth in a rather statesmanlike way, but now resumed his seat.

"Baby-Face is stupid, but Miyada depends on him," Noguchi began.

"You see, chief," Kimura interjected helpfully, "he gets his nickname because of his appearance. He's really quite goodlooking, and always well dressed. He's the one who takes care of the *sokaiya* work—you know, squeezing protection money from public companies by wrecking shareholders' meeting or threatening to. Ninja and I have been going through his record this morning. Miyada himself hasn't appeared in public for years, and almost certainly knows we've got a tap on his phones. If we let Baby-Face loose we think he'll go first to Miyada for orders, then to Carradine."

"Worth a try, anyway," said Noguchi. "Pull him in easy any time we like if it doesn't come off."

It was rare for Noguchi to endorse Kimura's recommendations, and Otani was impressed by their unanimity. "You're quite convinced that the haul came from the *Joon Hi*? The marker float was near, that much is clear from the photos. You say there was a man on deck watching the whole thing, Kimura, but he doesn't show up in any of the pictures. Did you see him, Ninja?" Noguchi shook his head.

"There was no chance, chief," Kimura pleaded. "Ninja had to concentrate on the pick-up with the telephoto lens. I had the binoculars. I could see the whole thing. I'll swear in any court that man was checking that nothing went wrong."

Otani nodded and gave a grunt of assent. "Very well. There's a clear possibility of a link to Carradine. You've persuaded me. Go ahead as you suggest. Ninja, it's up to you and your men not to lose sight of this, er, Baby-Face. Kimura, you'd better double and triplecheck the possibility of a motive for Carradine in doing away with the Baldwin woman. We've got to be very very sure of ourselves before I even think of putting this idea to the prosecutor . . ."

"OF COURSE!" The words came from Kimura almost as a howl, and even Noguchi turned his head to look at him in surprise. Kimura was beating his own forehead theatrically. "Why didn't I think of it before? Suppose he wasn't trying to kill Mrs Baldwin at all? Suppose the poison was intended for *somebody else*?"

Kimura beamed at the other two, delighted with himself and very obviously waiting for congratulations. Otani glanced at his watch again, and stood up. "I'm going to be late," he said to neither of them in particular, and crossed the room in the direction of his gold-braided uniform cap, hanging from the old-fashioned wooden coat and umbrella-stand near the door. As he passed him he looked sourly at Kimura who sat with the grin on his face fading to be replaced by an expression of puzzlement.

"The thought occurred to me some considerable time ago, Inspector. I was beginning to wonder when you'd get round to it. No, no, don't get up either of you. I suggest you stay here and discuss Kimura's brain-wave."

Chapter 13

Kinde are her answers

KIMURA HAD DURING THE PERIOD OF THEIR ACquaintance engaged in a variety of interesting and pleasurable activities in Ulla's flat, and although he was very grateful to her for engineering his meeting there with Lindy Kowalski, it was with an odd feeling of unease that he sat quietly on the sofa waiting for the last of those who had been in close proximity to Dorothy Baldwin when she died. The sofa in particular had lent itself to the achievement of some remarkable acrobatic feats on Ulla's part, and Kimura tenderly but unconsciously smoothed a cushion as he cleared his throat and rehearsed again in his imagination the lines on which he hoped the interview would develop.

He looked at his watch once more. Twelve forty-five. A perfectly reasonable hour for any married lady to be out shopping, and perhaps lunching in one of the many restaurants to be found on the top floor of any of the better department stores. The time mentioned had been twelve-thirty and Kimura had been in position after letting himself in with the key lent to him by Ulla for the past half-hour. His first preparatory fidgeting had been succeeded by a sense of annoyance with himself, and Kimura was beginning to entertain with a glimmer of relief the possibility that Mrs Kowalski might not turn up when the electronic chime of the Ansafone instrument sounded. He leapt up and lifted the receiver off the hook. "Hello? Mrs Kowalski?"

It was impossible to form any impression from the distorted and attenuated sound of the voice which responded, beyond the confirmation that the speaker was a foreign woman, and after bidding her heartily to come up, Kimura went to the door and opened it. He could hear that the lift was already in motion, and within a few seconds the doors across the small landing parted and Lindy Kowalski stepped out, manifestly nervous. Kimura opened the door to Ulla's flat wide and stood back. "It's very good of you to come, Mrs Kowalski," he said. "Come in, please."

She hesitated before doing so, but then stepped across the lobby and almost scuttled into the flat as Kimura closed the door behind her. "May I take your coat?" She nodded quickly and unbuttoned the light cloth coat she was wearing, then stood still, a small tooth working at her lower lip, until Kimura realised that she was waiting to have it removed for her. He crossed hastily and slipped it off her shoulders, noting the fragrance of her perfume.

Lindy Kowalski was thirty, but looked less. She was small, and her hair was so dark that from the back she might have passed as a Japanese woman. As Kimura laid the coat carefully over the back of the sofa, though, he was able to see that she was American through and through and extremely attractive into the bargain, in spite of the fact that she was much too heavily made up for the time of day. He had been too occupied to register her fully at the fatal party, and certainly not the fact that her eyes were of the smoky purplish blue that he had seen only rarely before, notably during a brief visit to Wales in his student days in Europe. The lower lip which she was still worrying at was full and soft, and underlying her present awkwardness there was the quiet arrogance of a woman who had quite clearly from her childhood been the prettiest girl around, conditioned to take for granted constant male attention.

"I'm Jiro Kimura. Won't you sit down?" Apart from identifying herself through the Ansafone, Lindy Kowalski had yet to utter a word, and it was still in silence that she looked Kimura up and down before nodding briefly and taking an easy-chair. She was wearing a cherry-red sweater which clung to well-shaped breasts, and a simply-cut skirt which she arranged with a deft flick over what Kimura had time to note were slender attractive thighs. Not really his type, Kimura concluded with some reluctance, but without doubt one who ten years before would have been a very strong candidate for an appearance in the centrefold of *Playboy* magazine.

"I must have been crazy to come here," she said at last. The voice was something of a disappointment emerging as it did from so glossy a package. It would have been appropriate in a high-school girl and might even have been described as cute, but was incongruously high and breathy for a mature woman. "Got a cigarette?"

The wheedling, 'please, Daddy' note reminded Kimura of the voice-overs for TV commercials, and he fumbled in his pocket, then half-withdrew his hand.

"Sure. Of course . . . that is, ah, Ulla doesn't care for cigarette smoke—"

"Fuck Ulla," came the immediate response, issuing strangely from the painted mouth, and Kimura hesitated no longer before producing a crumpled packet of Hi-Lites, then getting up from the sofa on which he had again settled himself as he became aware that Lindy Kowalski had no intention of leaning forward to take the proffered cigarette.

As Kimura snapped his lighter she seized his wrist to steady the flame. There was no guile in it, and Kimura decided that the gesture was completely automatic. Lindy Kowalski could no more shake off the settled habit of enslaving every man she met than she could allow her speaking voice to drop a tone to what must be its natural timbre. Kimura again found a second to reflect on the stroke of luck that, susceptible as he was, he could keep a cool head with women like Mrs Kowalski. Side by side with the thought was a flicker of human sympathy for Mr Kowalski.

He detached himself coolly and resumed his seat, leaning back and surveying the woman. Something was wrong. He now recalled having seen Lindy Kowalski at the Carradines' party, and indeed remembered her taking her place in the ranks of the Madrigal Circle. Although Kimura's own musical interests were of the most banal nature, his work on the Baldwin case had at least educated him into the supposition that madrigals were a somewhat specialised and recondite form, unlikely to appeal to the apparently self-centred yet superficial creature facing him. It was time to sort a few things out.

"I don't think you were crazy to come here," he observed mildly. "I think it's very fortunate that Ulla happens to be a friend of both of us." The gorgeous eyes were fixed on his, and Kimura saw if not intelligence then a kind of animal awareness in them. "I could have demanded this interview, Mrs Kowalski. But that would have meant going to the Consul-General and incidentally putting your husband in the picture."

"So? What would be the big deal in that?" The little-girl voice was uncertain.

"I told Ulla as much as she needed to know for me to persuade her to get you to meet me for an off-the-record conversation, Mrs Kowalski: I didn't tell her everything."

"What's to tell? And if this is off the record, do you have to be so formal? You can call me Lindy." She was winsome—again, and took an unnecessarily deep breath as she leaned back, obviously inviting him to eye her breasts.

With a considerable effort, Kimura averted his gaze. "Okay," he said. "I'll lay it on the line. I am a police officer as you well know. You may be able to help me. I can't guarantee that we can keep you out of this, but I *can* probably spare you a good deal of embarrassment. It's information about *you* that can stay off the record. You're hoping that now, and that's why you agreed to come here"

"Will you quit talking mysterious? Ulla said you wanted to tell me something about Pat Carradine. That's not embarrassing. Angie knows we're screwing and so does Duane—gee, they get it together themselves now and then. There's nothing much else to do in this dumb town, for God's sake." Lindy took a hungry pull at her cigarette, then stubbed it out so fiercely that the paper split at the bend. "Doesn't have anything to do with Dorothy."

The readiness with which Lindy Kowalski referred to her relationship with Carradine took the wind out of Kimura's sails, more especially as the information came as a surprise to him. Ulla had made one or two darkly ambiguous remarks about the Carradines but had said nothing about the Kowalskis beyond the mere mention of their names in connection with the group of joggers who met early each morning. She must however have calculated the most effective way to set up Kimura's meeting with Lindy: for in asking Ulla's help he had merely suggested that the formality of striking the American woman's name off the list of possible suspects could be achieved much more simply after an apparently casual encounter than by going through the tedious rigmarole of an official request to interview a person with diplomatic status.

The totally unexpected bonus he had already received and Kimura's lingering puzzlement over the personality of Lindy Kowalski prompted him to abandon his tactical plan and go ahead off the cuff. He knew he was a mere amateur as compared with Otani in keeping a poker face, but did his best nevertheless to dissemble his surprise. "It may have more than you imagine to do with the murder of Dorothy Baldwin. Besides, what would be the point of my telling you that you sleep with Patrick Carradine?"

Kimura left the question hanging, while he looked at his watch ostentatiously. Then he leaned forward and stared at her, harsh and unyielding in what he thought of as his Perry Mason persona. "You haven't been a member of this Madrigal Circle very long," he announced flatly. "You were introduced to it by Donald Schaeffer. Does your husband know you're sleeping with him too?"

This time Lindy Kowalski stirred uneasily in her chair. Kimura could almost hear the shifting of gears in her thought processes as she tried to react to his bombshell. "Who says I am?" she said at last.

It was all that Kimura could do to prevent himself from mopping his forehead with relief. Time enough to congratulate himself on his brilliance later. "Never mind that," he snapped. "Let me just say that I know a good deal about Donald Schaeffer. I also know that you have very little interest in all that madrigal stuff. It was just a neat way to see him without calling attention to the situation. How did you meet him in the first place?"

"Look, uh . . . you say Duane need not know anything about this . . . about me meeting you here?"

The cute voice was shy and plaintive, and Kimura sat back in triumph, allowing himself to give her a smile of infinite understanding and sympathy. "Not as long as you answer my questions honestly and simply," he said graciously. "Ulla will certainly not mention anything about the matter."

Lindy gulped, the expression of guilt on her pretty face naive, like that of a small child caught out in a fib. "I'll just die, I know I shall." The words came out almost as a wail, and Kimura shook his head, a stern but kindly elder brother.

"Relax," he suggested. "There won't be too many questions. First, how did you meet Donald Schaeffer?"

Lindy looked down at her perfectly varnished nails. "At a party," she whispered. "He just . . . Gee, I can't explain it. I just flipped for him."

Kimura nodded sagely, a new thought occurring to him. "It's not really your husband you're keeping it quiet from, is it, Lindy? It's Carradine."

She looked up at him as though he were performing an incredible conjuring trick. Her whole body seemed to crumple, and then she dropped her head again.

"How long have you been married, Lindy?"

"Seven years," came the whispered reply.

"And when did you and your husband agree to—you know—go your own ways, ah, sexually?"

Lindy blushed prettily and somewhat unexpectedly. "Pretty much from the start, I guess. Well, for Heaven's sake, we met at a swap party in Santa Barbara in the first place."

It was all becoming a little too much for Kimura, but he pressed on bravely and with an apparent confidence which at least seemed to impress Lindy. "Right. So when you came here to Kobe, let's see now, just under a year ago, it didn't take you long to figure the Carradines as the sort of swingers you might get it on with."

"Get it together," she corrected him absent-mindedly.

"Right." Kimura made a mental note of the idiom, which he thought he had reproduced accurately from an earlier remark of hers.

"But Carradine is unexpectedly possessive where you're concerned?"

"Right. Oh boy, you said it." Lindy nodded vigorously as though endorsing a comment on some perfectly ordinary matter, her former embarrassment no longer evident. "Why, after the first few times he didn't want the others in the same room even. Can you imagine? Then he started getting real jealous about other people, even Duane. It's gotten so it isn't any fun any more." Kimura had read paperback books about people like Lindy Kowalski, but the experience of actually talking to one was new and disconcerting.

"Donald Schaeffer is different, though," he suggested. Lindy Kowalski said nothing. She had no need to. It was obvious to Kimura that she was totally, hopelessly in love with the objectionable young man; and though Kimura was himself viewing her with mounting distaste he nevertheless found himself wondering what she could see in Schaeffer in comparison with the wealthy, handsome and influential Carradine.

"So Schaeffer suggested that you should join the Madrigal Circle," he said rather heavily. "When was that?"

Lindy nibbled at her lower lip, a little girl trying to remember her eight times table. "Three, four weeks ago," she said. "And the members meet for rehearsal each week at the Carradines: but Pat always makes it his business to stay away from home those evenings.

"I know—he told me. All the same, I suppose Mrs Carradine is around occasionally. Don't you think he might have found out about you and Donald Schaeffer?"

The beautiful eyes opened wide in horror. "You mean—Jesus, you mean . . . Don? That maybe Angie said something to Pat and he checked and found out and was trying to *kill* him? And that Dorothy was . . ." She trailed to a bewildered silence, wrestling to comprehend the inconceivable.

Kimura pursed his lips judiciously. There were two paths open, clearly signposted, and he hesitated over the choice of direction. "Do you really think that Carradine is so jealous of any other man in your, ah, life that he'd actually try to *kill* such a person?"

Lindy blew out a long breath, then wrung her hands. "Well, he sure *said* it often enough," she began haltingly. "But, you know, the way people do. Not like you really mean it. Yeah, he's crazy about me I guess, but, like, I can imagine him beating Don up or something, but, gee . . ." Kimura took some comfort from the fact that, idioms aside, her English vocabulary was more limited than his.

"How much do you see of Carradine, Lindy? How frequently, I mean?"

She screwed up her face. "Every goddam day. Not every night—we fuck maybe two, three times a week. But he gets so mad if I don't show for the jogging every damn morning, even after . . ."

Lindy broke off and Kimura suddenly remembered Ulla using exactly the same phrase. He now realised what she must have meant. "Apart from, that is, sex and jogging, do you see Carradine much? I mean, do you ever have a meal at a restaurant with him? Ever been to his office? Does he ever talk about his business with you?" Lindy flapped a hand defensively in the face of Kimura's barrage of questions, and he paused to let her reply.

"We don't go out together," she said primly. "Duane wouldn't allow it, the jogging's different. There's a whole gang of us. I don't know a thing about Pat's business." She sighed glumly. "No, I guess it's just the screwing. And the jogging."

Kimura coud not help himself. "It seems somehow strange that your husband doesn't mind you going to bed with Carradine but won't allow you to go out with him."

"He's a *diplomat*," she said with a touch of pride. "People like us have to keep up appearances."

"So you don't talk about Carradine's business with him," Kimura persisted. "You really don't know anything about his activities?"

"I keep *telling* you. You're getting me all confused. First you say Pat tried to kill Don, and now you keep asking me all this dumb stuff about his *business*?"

Kimura stared at her coldly. "I didn't say he tried to kill Donald," he murmured. "You did. As a matter of fact it struck me that he might have been trying to kill you."

Chapter 14

Construe my meaning

THOSE OF OTANI'S FELLOW MEMBERS WHO HAD ALready arrived at the Kobe South Rotary Club were suitably impressed when he led Ambassador Atsugi over to the registration table and signed him in as his guest for the regular weekly luncheon meeting. It had come as something of a surprise to Otani to discover that Atsugi was a Rotarian like himself: although he was certainly more than distinguished enough for admission to their ranks, Otani would have thought him a little too outgoing to be happy among them. His brief puzzlement was soon cleared up when Atsugi explained that he had been inducted into Rotarianism in the United States. Otani had often commented to Hanae on the demonstrative, hail-fellow-well-met characteristics of the visiting American Rotarians who quite commonly put in an appearance at the Kobe South Club, handing over the presentation pennants from their home clubs to add to the considerable collection displayed each week on portable screens, and receiving the colourful gold-fringed Kobe South pennant in exchange.

It seemed that Atsugi had been admitted with exceptional speed into the huge and immensely prestigious Osaka Club, and Otani beamed proprietorially as he introduced the Foreign Ministry man to his particular friends before the bell rang to summon them all into the private dining-room at the New Port Hotel for the hurriedly served meal which Otani very seldom enjoyed. That week it was chicken à la king yet again, followed by the inevitable scoop of icecream and demi-tasse of coffee.

Atsugi was amiability itself throughout the meal, and listened with ostensibly benign attentiveness to the guest speaker, a Shinto priest who dwelt optimistically on the fact that the demand for special rites at the more important shrines in the region had been steadily increasing for several years, and managed to work in a few sly references to the continuing controversy over whether the Japanese Constitution should or should not be revised. Like every other middle-aged or elderly man in the room Otani was perfectly well aware of the implications of the priest's bland remarks, and exchanged a glance with Atsugi as he recalled the time when, still in his teens, he had been marched with the other newly commissioned junior officers in the Imperial Navy under the mighty looming *torii* gateway into the precincts of the great Yasukuni Shrine not far from the Imperial Palace in Tokyo; there to dedicate themselves to the spirits of the war dead and to express the hope that they too would be privileged to lay down their lives in the service of the Emperor. The man from the Foreign Ministry reached for a toothpick, delicately removed it from its paper wrapper and applied it thoughtfully, shielding his mouth politely with his free hand.

The applause at the end was of a ragged quality, with old Moriyama predictably clapping loudest of all, glaring round defiantly at his neighbours as he did so, while many others sat on their hands with equal ostentatiousness. Otani had a feeling that remarks would be made to the club secretary about the choice of such a controversial speaker. The following week would be uneventful enough, though, since it was announced that the principal guest would be the hereditary grand master of one of the schools of the tea ceremony, and he would be unlikely to offend anyone, except possibly the income tax authorities.

"One-thirty precisely," said Atsugi as the little bell was struck and they stood up, pushing back their chairs. "You're very good time-keepers here. The Osaka Club sometimes runs on as long as five minutes."

Shaking his head sorrowfully at the thought of such Babylonian excesses, Otani ushered his guest out of the private room and through to the main hotel lobby. "It's a pity it's raining," he said. "I had thought of suggesting that you might be interested to visit the artificial island in the harbour here. Where they staged the Portopia Exposition a couple of years ago. You get an excellent view of the shipping in the harbour from the special train, but . . ."

"And you wanted to point out the *Joon Hi* to me? It's really not necessary, Superintendent. Why don't we have a quiet cup of coffee over there in the lounge instead?"

The big man pointed to the area where light refreshments were served, and actually cupped a hand round Otani's elbow to pilot him there, just like a real American Rotarian. Nothing more was said until the coffee had been ordered and set before them by a very young waitress in a plain pink dress, white ankle socks and tennis shoes. Then Atsugi looked at Otani quizzically as he tore open a packet of sugar and dumped the contents into his coffee. "Are you sure about this?"

"Sure enough," Otani replied simply.

Atsugi sat back and spoke in an almost professorial manner. "It was good of you to ring me and mention your intention. I suggested we should meet somewhere privately because even on the confidential phone line there must always be some slight possibility of leaks. Those pictures you showed me on the way from the station are certainly extremely interesting. And you tell me that Inspector Noguchi's original informer has put the finger on that particular ship too. An arrest of a ship is very sensitive business, though. Especially one with a South Korean registration. I can't stop you. The harbour police are under your jurisdiction, and if the head of Customs is prepared to support you then you're within your rights. All the same, Superintendent, I feel obliged to warn you that if you can't make the charges stick you'll be in very big trouble indeed."

Otani looked at him quietly, taking his time over replying. He was fairly sure that Atsugi would have informed himself about the connection between the ship and Carradine's business interests even though Otani had not himself mentioned it. He was equally sure that Atsugi would prefer him to take no action over the *Joon Hi*, though he was in doubt about the diplomat's motives. He did not strike Otani as being the sort of man who would shrink from a mere political fuss; and even the Korean Ambassador in Tokyo could scarcely protest very convincingly if solid evidence could be produced to demonstrate beyond question that the drugs were brought to Japan on board a freighter flying their flag.

Otani was now in no doubt that it could. He decided to put his cards on the table.

"Look, Ambassador," he said, "we've caught the small men. We have enough to make life quite difficult for the gang boss they work for. But I want more. I *want* publicity. I want the masters of freighters, the captains of aircraft, anybody in authority to realise that if they connive at drug smuggling we're going to throw the book at them. Massive fines, impounding, the whole lot."

Atsugi finished his coffee, pulling a face as he realised that it was cold. "I admire your determination," he said quietly. "But if you'll forgive my saying so aren't you getting delusions of grandeur? You don't really think you're going to be able to put a stop to drug trafficking, do you? Don't think me rude, and don't think I'm underestimating the importance of having heavy penalties and applying them. You're an expert in your job, and it's not for me to tell you how to do it. However, you know that we have some extremely tricky negotiations going with the Koreans at the moment. I've taken you into my confidence—"

"Have you?"

Atsugi looked at Otani hard. "So far as I can. Have *you* done the same?"

"What do you mean?" Otani's reply was so blandly innocent that it made Atsugi laugh out loud.

"Oh come on, Superintendent. You're trying to flush out a murderer at least as much as you're intending more or less singlehandedly to wipe out sin from the face of the earth." It was very unusual for anyone to speak to Otani in such a way, and he was taken aback. Atsugi hadn't finished, though. "It's curious, isn't it," he continued in a perfectly friendly manner. "Those petty gangsters your men picked up. Paradoxically, they're much more dangerous killers in effect than the conventional murderer who picks out a single victim and—" With a meaty hand he made a sawing gesture at his own throat, accompaying it with a quite revolting noise which made Otani grin in spite of himself. "No, I mean it. The social effects of drugs. Terrible. You're quite right to take it seriously. All the same, I strongly suspect that you have some complicated idea about how to get your hands on a certain prominent British business man. I don't blame you in the least," he added with an air of fair-mindedness. "It is an intriguing affair."

"I must say," Otani remarked thoughtfully, "you're a very different proposition from Ambassador Tsunematsu. How is he, by the way?"

Atsugi winked. "Hot, I should imagine. Still, he's due home after his three years in Africa pretty soon. Then he'll retire and get a nice advisory job with one of the big trading companies. Superintendent, you're evading the issue."

Otani's swarthy face was a mask, but his voice when he spoke revealed his good humour. "I know," he said. "I've been sitting here accepting the justice of what you say. We theorise a lot, you see, in my sort of job. Try out dozens of ideas, most of them very silly and far-fetched. I could no more take you into my confidence, as you put it, than you can take me into yours. What I mean is that it would be literally impossible to pin down all the thoughts floating around in my head in words. You probably know as much about the facts, such as they are, as I do."

"Try me," suggested Atsugi, and Otani sat quietly for a while while the big, breezy man contemplated the small, compact police officer in the conservative dark suit sitting opposite him.

"Facts," said Otani at last. "A woman murdered by

poisoning in the private home of the head of a foreign trading firm which happens to be the agent for a Korean shipping line. Extensive enquiries cannot throw up the slightest trace of a motive, but as always reveal some very odd relationships and situations. Poison used could well have been supplied by a Korean crook, but might equally have been obtained elsewhere. Informer suggests that the head of the foreign firm and host at the party where the poison was administered is running an important drug smuggling operation. Informer provides accurate information about pick-up methods, which enables my men to intercept a big consignment and net some minor gangsters. They also bring back compelling evidence that the drugs came from a ship belonging to the line which the foreign businessman represents . . . back to the beginning. Facts, you wanted. Well, there they are."

"Thank you," said Atsugi. "It is, as you imply, an impressive and suggestive accumulation of evidence. All circumstantial as far as your chief suspect is concerned, though. Wouldn't you say?" With the last few words Atsugi stood up and Otani followed suit. "I must go," he said.

"What's your advice?" Otani was as surprised to hear himself asking the question as Atsugi appeared to be on having it addressed to him.

He spread out his hands palms upwards, arm bent at the elbow in another of his alien gestures, and raised his luxuriant eyebrows. "It's not for me to tell you how to do your job," he said. "Since you ask me, though, I'd be inclined to hold your action for perhaps, oh, twenty-four hours or so." Atsugi pulled pensively at the end of his nose. "Did you say you have a tail on the man Carradine?"

"I didn't say. To tell you the truth, I don't know,"

Otani admitted. "I know we're keeping an eye on the boss of the villains we arrested."

They ambled together towards the main entrance of the hotel. "Well," Atsugi continued, "it seems to me that *if* your theory is right, then your man ought to be getting rather worried by now. I suppose he might do something which would give you a real lead? It's just an idea, of course. I'm an innocent in these matters." He smiled broadly as Otani glaced at him quizzically. "Thank you for lunch, Superintendent," he said. "Let's keep in touch." It had not stopped raining, and they stood together in the shelter of the portico while the Foreign Ministry man unfurled the umbrella he had retrieved from the rack and touched the button to make it pop up. Then he waved airily as he swung off in the direction of Sannomiya Station. Otani had been intending to go the same way, but he hesitated, then put up his own umbrella and instead headed down towards the harbour, where he spent some time in the office of the Head of Customs, including several minutes studying the *Joon Hi* with the aid of a pair of borrowed binoculars.

Chapter 15

So quicke, so hot, so mad

OTANI WAS NOT A HEAVY SLEEPER, BUT EVEN SO the ringing of the telephone extension in the upstairs room took some time to rouse him. Although since reaching his present seniority it was comparatively rare for him to be disturbed at night, Hanae never failed to put the phone in place with a pencil and note-pad on the smooth tatami mat near Otani's side of the bedding she took out of the big cupboard and unrolled for them each night. In fact she woke first, and had half-sprawled over him in an attempt to reach the receiver when he came to and picked it up himself.

Otani grunted a response and listened to the perfunctory apologies of Ninja Noguchi at the other end of the line, peering at the fluorescent hands of the watch which was also lying on the tatami mat beside the phone. It was just before two-thirty in the morning. Noguchi continued to talk for some time, after which Otani put one question to him, and listened quietly to the answer. "Very well. I'll be ready," was all he said then, before replacing the receiver and lying back, rubbing the sleep from his eyes.

Hanae had said nothing, but enough light was diffused through the soft white paper of the shoji screens which covered the window glass for him to see that her eyes were open. He propped himself up on one elbow, then leant over and kissed her gently on the forehead. Then on an impulse he drew open the neck of the cotton yukata she always wore in bed and nuzzled at her breast.

She stirred and her voice was no more than a whisper. "You've got to go out," she said, making it a statement rather than a question.

"Yes," he said, and kissed her again. "The car will be here for me in a few minutes." As he drew away she reached up and hugged him with a sudden fierceness, and Otani detached himself with some surprise. "Don't worry, Ha-chan," he said. "I won't be long."

He rolled out of bed and moved quietly about the room as he pulled on some clothes. After her initial reaction Hanae too got up, straightened the folds of her yukata about her, and switched on the small bedside lamp which stood on the matting at her side. She watched uneasily as Otani rummaged in a drawer and produced a dark sweater he scarcely ever wore, pulling it over his naked torso. He had already put on a pair of dark trousers. Hanae knew him too well to ask where he was going. She just watched in silence until she caught his eye. Then he grinned, shamefaced but excited. "Really, I mean it," he said. "That was Ninja Noguchi. Something interesting has happened and he thought I might like to join him."

"Do you have to go yourself?" Hanae stared at his

unusual getup. "You're not going to do anything dangerous, are you?"

Otani grinned again, crossed quickly to her and took her by the shoulders. "What, at my time of life? Not likely. Ninja's going to take me for a little cruise round the harbour," he said. "We shall have young Migishima with us to take care of the two old gentlemen. But in any case, we're only going to look at something, then we'll be back." He gave her a little shake then released her and went over to the bedside, picked up his watch and slipped it on his wrist. "Two thirty-five," he said. "Let's see, I should be back. oh, by about five at the latest. You go back to bed, and I'll come back beside you very quietly and . . ." He leered at her in the style of a comic seducer and she nodded, a small shy smile on her face in spite of the fact that her lips were pressed together with nervous tension. Hanae knew him in his rare manic phases, and realised that there was not the slightest prospect of dissuading him from this mysterious project which seemed to have filled him with schoolboyish glee.

In the quietude of the night the sound of the car drawing up outside the house was very noticeable and Hanae philosophically led the way downstairs, thus enabling Otani unnoticed by her to slip his regulation pistol into the inside of the wind-cheater he put on over his sweater. He had already transferred his warrant card from his wallet to the back pocket of his slacks.

When he reached the bottom of the stairs he saw that Hanae had already looked out a pair of rubber-soled canvas shoes that he wore occasionally when they went for walks in the hills behind the house at weekends and had set them ready for him in the tiny entrance hall. She knelt with artless grace on the rather worn tatami mat, absent-mindedly making a minute adjustment to the flower arrangement in the flat ceramic bowl in the alcove at her side as Otani sat on the step and put the shoes on.

As he stood and reached out a hand to unfasten the simple screw lock which secured the sliding outer door she put both hands on the mat in front of her and bowed. "*Itte irasshai*. Go forth and return, she murmured. The phrase was the same conventional formula she used to him every day, but Otani heard the catch in her voice.

"Don't worry," he insisted. Then, cheerily, "Well, I'm off. Back soon." A rattle as he opened the door, another as he slid it shut behind him, and he was outside in the fresh night air.

He saw at once with satisfaction that it was his personal Toyota Police Special which was waiting in the unmade roadway outside, with his own driver Tomita grinning toothily as he stood holding the rear door open for him. Otani acknowledged his greeting and settled himself in the car. It was not until they were approaching the outskirts of Kobe fifteen minutes later that it occurred to him to enquire the reason for Tomita's availability. The diminutive Tomita was the senior man in the pool of headquarters drivers, but having attached himself to the Superintendent for the past several years he usually put his name on the same roster as Otani himself. "I heard there might be something in the wind tonight, sir," he admitted in high good humour. "So I decided to sleep in the emergency room just in case you needed me. Didn't want to take the risk of having Sato drive you."

Otani shook his head ruefully. It was true that when Sato took the wheel occasionally in Tomita's absence Otani found himself closing his eyes in silent prayer from time to time and that he greatly preferred Tomita's sedate style; even though Tomita did have something of a genius for getting lost while in the process unerringly heading for any traffic jam within a five mile radius of their destination. What rather bothered him about Tomita's remark was the confirmation it provided of his long-standing suspicion that as officer commanding the entire prefectural force he, Otani, was usually the last to hear about anything interesting that cropped up.

"I see. Well, Tomita, I take it you know exactly where we're supposed to go?" The moon was almost at the full, and though it would soon be setting it provided a good deal of illumination. They had still not reached the centre of the city, and the area through which they were passing was dimly lit. Through the car window Otani could see ragged shreds of clouds against a sky which was now mainly clear.

The small head with its short, bristly haircut bobbed in front of him. "Oh yes, sir. The Inspector was very particular that I should stop in an alley near the entrance to Pier Three, just round from the clock tower."

Otani sat back in silence for the remainder of the drive, pleasurable excitement warding off any return of drowsiness even in the quiet enclosed world of the police car dimly lit by the eerie green glow of the instrument panel and the continuous background whisper of the static from the radio interrupted by the occasional crackle of a voice. It had been a long time since he had last sampled the experience of a night patrol drive, he reflected, and made a mental note to arrange something of the kind before the end of the year.

The port area was pretty well deserted, except for one pier which was a blaze of light from arc-lamps revealing a gang of men swarming like hellish imps over a construction project, the showers of sparks from welding torches constituting small and beautiful local infernos of their own. Beyond, nothing could be seen of the harbour itself until they were clear of the work and Otani's eyes again became adjusted to the night. Then the red, green and white riding lights on the vessels at anchor could be seen, with the upperworks of some of them dimly lit.

They passed the Customs House and after only a very brief hesitation Tomita swung the wheel to the left and brought the car to a halt about fifty metres down a narrow access road. Then he stopped the engine and turned off the head and sidelights. Tomita had no time to get out and open the door for Otani. It was opened from the outside and the eager head of Migishima ducked in. "Good morning, sir," he said. Otani was distinctly startled, for at first all he could see in the dimness was teeth and the whites of Migishima's eyes. Then the head was withdrawn and Otani climbed out, after which it registered with him that Migishima had blackened his face in the manner of commando raiders in war films.

Otani denied Migishima the pleasure of being invited to explain himself, and merely acknowledged his greeting curtly. "Where's the Inspector?" he then asked.

"I'm to take you to him, sir. Oh, and he suggested that Tomita should turn the car back into this same position, in case . . ."

Otani suppressed the urge to ask the obvious question. It seemed in the highest degree improbable that they, the police, might find it necessary to make a rapid getaway. "Well, you'd better tell him, then," was all he said before strolling forward a few paces and sniffing the air. Although he had spent much of his working life within less than a kilometre of the harbour, it was easy to forget the maritime basis of Kobe's economy, and Otani enjoyed the occasions when his professional concerns brought him near the water.

Very soon Migishima was back at his side, towering over him and obviously longing to enter into a conspiratorial relationship. Otani had an old-fashioned sense of hierarchy, though, and while he quite liked the young man he had no intention of discussing the business in hand with him before hearing what Noguchi had to say. He decided to compromise by exhibiting a friendly interest in Migishima's domestic arrangements: he and Hanae had after all attended the reception following his marriage to former Woman Patrolman Terauchi, now Woman Detective Junko Migishima.

"I understand that your wife has now received approval for her transfer to the Criminal Investigation Section. I hope you are both pleased about that?"

Migishima nodded his comically blackened face vigorously. "Yes, sir, thank you, sir. She is very grateful to you, sir. The first woman ever to serve under Inspector Sakamoto. Great honour, sir." They rounded a bend as Otani peered up sidelong at his escort. Ahead of them was a wicket gate with a uniformed policeman standing outside.

"It was nothing to do with me, Migishima," he said mildly. "All the same, give her my congratulations."

The uniformed man at the gate betrayed no surprise on seeing the commander of the prefectural force in such casual dress, but passed them through the gate with a smart salute all the same, so he must have known who Otani was. The wicket gate gave directly on to a jetty, and it took Otani a few seconds to make out the bulky form of Noguchi in the shadows cast by the wall. He crossed quietly to him and Noguchi nodded by way of greeting.

It occurred to Otani later that there was no particular need for them to converse in an undertone. The *Joon Hi* was anchored some hundreds of metres out, and there was not the slightest possibility of their voices carrying that far. Nevertheless, he found himself speaking in little more than a whisper and Noguchi's habitual terse growl was throttled back to a hoarse rumble.

"You're sure he's on board? No doubt at all?"

Noguchi nodded again. "He's there all right. Good thing you ordered the tail. First man followed him home from his office. Nothing unusual. About sevenish. Handed over to his relief at ten. Reported that situation seemed normal in the apartment. Signs of movement, but nothing special. Certain amount of coming and going at the block. Recognised that guy on the TV, whatsisname, Adachi, come back about nine with his tart. One visitor to the top floor apartment. Foreign woman. Small, dark. Bit of a dish, he said. Arrived about nine-thirty by taxi. Still there, so far as we know."

Even Noguchi was in dark clothes that night, though Otani was somewhat relieved to note that only Migishima, who was now sidling closer and closer to them in a transparent attempt to listen in, had daubed what smelt like shoe polish on his face. "So it was the night duty man who managed to get up to the balcony, then?"

"Yeah. Thought he was in for a private show," Noguchi muttered, never taking his eyes from the night glasses which he had trained on the Korean freighter. "Drinks, soft lights, big guy, Carradine, in sexy clinch with little dark bird. In walks tall blonde, none of them turn a hair. End of show, though. Little one suddenly starts jabbering and crying at the same time, the other two obviously thunderstruck. Big conference, then he's on the phone. Worried. Goes out."

"It's a good job our man was able to get down again in time to tail him," worried Otani.

"Tore himself away," said Noguchi sardonically. "Boring, following Carradine to his office wondering what the girls were up to by then . . . anyway, had the sense to radio for help. Carradine stayed at his office for about an hour. Meantime I got word and got hold of young Migishima here . . .''

''Inspector Kimura's at the Carradine office now, sir,'' Migishima interjected helpfully. ''Looking for incriminating documents.'' Otani's mouth twitched at the melodramatic phrase, but he nodded gravely. ''We—that is, Inspector Noguchi was on his way there with me driving when we got the word on the radio that the suspect was heading for the harbour.''

Noguchi lowered the binoculars and rubbed his eyes before raising them again. ''Shut up, son,'' he said not unkindly, and Migishima subsided.

Otani was becoming slightly impatient. ''Yes, yes. I've heard some of this already. It was very fortunate you were able to get down here before him. You say he showed his bonded area pass to the Customs guard and went in quite openly, though. He has a perfectly legitimate connection with the *Joon Hi* although I must say, hardly at two o'clock in the morning . . .'' Otani's voice trailed away as Noguchi lowered the glasses again, ignoring him.

''Well, what about it? He's been on board nearly half an hour. We going over to have a look?'' He took Otani's agreement for granted, leading the way over to a flight of stone steps cut into the jetty wall. A dinghy bobbed about below, tied up by a short length of rope to an iron ring let into the wall. Migishima went ahead and held up a steady arm which, after a moment's hesitation, Otani took as he stepped gingerly into the little boat, grateful for Hanae's foresight in getting the rubber-soled shoes out for him.

''I still think it might have been useful to have Kimura along,'' he murmured to Noguchi when the boat listed heavily with his arrival on the scene. "I know Carradine speaks Japanese, but he's bound to be using English on the ship." Again Noguchi ignored him, and the thought flashed suddenly into Otani's mind that they were all simply humouring him by bringing him along at all, and that they probably felt they would do a lot better without him. He clamped his jaws tight and sat still as Migishima manoeuvred the dinghy away from the jetty wall with surprising delicacy and then with a few powerful pulls on the oars set them moving towards the freighter.

Their progress was far from soundless, but the creaking and splashing of the oars was lost as they approached the *Joon Hi* and Migishima edged them round the stern of the ship and into the shadow of the hull at the other side, since a steady stream of water was pouring noisily into the sea from a bilge-pump outlet some feet above the water-line. Almost over their heads was a wooden painters' cradle, and the smell of fresh paint overlaid the foetid, sulphurous odour of the water.

Migishima edged them along to the companionway, to the bottom of which two dinghies similar to their own were tied up. "I wonder why there are two?" mused Otani quietly to Noguchi. "One for Carradine . . . oh, of course, the other one belongs to the ship itself. Well, what do you suggest we should do?"

Noguchi looked at him in silence for some time before replying. "Only two things we can do," he then said with an air of slight surprise. "Push off out of sight and tail him back when he leaves. Or go on board and ask him what the hell he thinks he's up to. You were planning to arrest the ship anyway. Do it with him on it. That's why I phoned you."

Otani hesitated only briefly, having had plenty of time during the drive from his house to go over the pros and cons of immediate action. He knew from his conversations in the Customs office that the ship carried a crew of about twenty including officers, and that most of the crewmen had been on shore leave for several days. If Carradine had as seemed obvious gone on board for confidential discussions there was unlikely to be anybody about on deck at that hour. The element of surprise might indeed be a useful weapon for them. "Right," he said crisply. "Tie the boat up, Migishima. We'll all go aboard."

Migishima was clearly in a state of barely-suppressed euphoria and Otani's own adrenalin flow made it difficult for him to maintain his habitual outward calm, but Noguchi heaved himself out of the little boat and started to climb the companionway with no more apparent concern than if he had been mounting the steps to a restaurant where he was proposing to enjoy a quiet meal. Otani followed, the heavy bulk of the gun thumping against his ribs with each step, and Migishima brought up the rear.

There were a few low-wattage lamps burning here and there, but no sign of life on deck. It looked as if the loading of return cargo was pretty well complete, since the hatches were battened down and neatly covered by roped tarpaulins. The Harbourmaster had in any case confirmed when Otani rang him from the Customs office that the *Joon Hi* was due to sail in a couple of days after the completion of minor repairs and repainting.

The three men moved carefully along towards the bridge, passing what were evidently crew and officers' quarters. All the cabins appeared to be in darkness except for the area immediately aft of the bridge, where light came from two portholes. Migishima fidgeted in an agony of anticipation as Noguchi and Otani each moved quietly up to one of them and glanced inside. It was he, not Otani, who noticed the sudden rigidity in Noguchi's stance, and the grey, sick pallor that came into his battered face clearly visible in the light spilling through the glass.

Chapter 16

Down from Above

THE CABIN WAS QUITE SMALL; PERHAPS THREE METRES square, and looked to Otani as though it might normally be used as some kind of dining-room. A fixed bench, padded and covered with shiny brown plastic, ran along the length of one side, and there was a fairsized table, bolted to the forward bulkhead, which had a hinged leaf so that it could be stowed economically when not in use. Apart from the door which opened on to the deck on which the police officers were standing, there was another, interior door which Otani supposed gave admittance to a galley or possibly to the master's personal quarters. The undrawn curtains were of some kind of synthetic material in a bright orange colour, and constituted the sole element of decoration in the cabin.

Two men were seated side by side on the bench, about two feet apart and turned slightly towards each other. The table was up, and on its surface were scattered a few papers, largely obscured by Carradine's forearm on which he was leaning as he bent forward to speak earnestly to his companion. It was the first time Otani had seen the big Englishman of whom he had heard so much, and he looked him over with some care, before turning his attention to the other man.

He was much smaller than Carradine, but looked wiry and compact in a way which reminded Otani briefly of Kimura. His features appeared entirely Japanese to Otani, who guessed his age must be somewhere in the early to middle thirties. He was sitting back in an attitude of apparent relaxation, listening quietly and occasionally tapping the table top with the end of the pencil he held in his left hand. The coarse material of his dark blue jersey sleeve contrasted sharply with the soft, expensive cashmere of Carradine's jacket, but his whole demeanour was somehow more authoritative than the Englishman's. The black intelligent eyes were watchful and steady, and the only thing about the man which would mark him off in the streets of Kobe from a purposeful, composed Japanese of the same age group was his haircut, which was of severe military style, clipped high above his ears.

Otani was indulging himself in a moment of self-congratulation on having pinpointed the matter of the haircut when he became aware of a persistent pulling at his sleeve and a whispered "Superintendent. Sir." in his ear. He moved back in some irritation but before having a chance to attend to and possibly rebuke Migishima he saw the reason for the interruption. Noguchi was standing stockstill at the rail, his head bowed and his eyes closed, hands folded in a curiously peaceful attitude. It was only the ghastly pallor of his face which gave cause for concern but the moment Otani looked at his old friend he knew without a trace of doubt that the man in the cabin with Carradine must be his son, Hayashi.

He moved quickly to Noguchi's side and grasped him by one massive upper arm. "Ninja. I know. I know all about everything. Don't say anything. You must go. Now. We'll all go back to the car. We must think about this." Slowly the heavy head was raised, slowly the eyelids opened to reveal an expression of such infinite pain that Otani was himself almost unmanned, while Migishima was standing by gazing at them both, bewildered and utterly at a loss.

After staring unseeingly at Otani for several seconds like someone under the influence of a narcotic drug, Noguchi almost imperceptibly shook his head. "No," he whispered. "Got to go through with it." With a huge effort he straightened himself up, and it was as though shutters went down behind his eyes, barring to Otani any further evidence of his inner emotions.

Otani shook his own head firmly, summoning up all his impressive natural authority. "You will do as I order you, Inspector Noguchi," he said, and although he kept his voice as low as possible it was filled with power. "You will return immediately to the dinghy and Detective Migishima will escort you to my car where you will wait for your instructions." Then he turned to Migishima. "The Inspector is unwell," he said. "Escort him to my car. As soon as you get the dinghy to open water, use your walkie-talkie. We're probably out of radio contact this side, because of the bulk of the ship. I want two armed, uniformed men and the senior duty Customs officer to join me here as soon as possible. You come back too."

Noguchi was still standing upright, apparently in control of himself and now glaring defiantly at Otani. He opened his mouth to protest, but Otani spoke first. "It's an order, Ninja. I'm sorry." The very mildness of his tone seemed to penetrate to Noguchi more effectively than Otani's earlier peremptoriness. The heavy shoulders sagged slightly and the fire went out of his eyes. Then he turned and moved away quietly in the direction of the companionway, Migishima preceding him and Otani bringing up the rear, determined to see him safely into the dinghy before resuming his vigil outside the cabin.

It was while he was standing at the head of the companionway watching Noguchi negotiate the last few steps, with Migishima already in the boat and extending an arm to help him, that Otani all at once experienced an animal awareness of a presence behind him. He whirled round to see the man Hayashi no more than a few feet away, with the tall Englishman behind him. "So. I *did* hear something. What do you think you're doing?"

The voice was calm, the accent and timbre that of a native born, well-educated Japanese. In a reaction of protectiveness towards Noguchi, Otani approached the two men. They were well away from the rail and it seemed probable in view of their concentration on himself that they were unaware that he was not alone. "Just looking around," Otani said, with as much composure as he could manage.

Hayashi raised an eyebrow. "At this hour of the night? All right, who are you?"

Otani had often over the years teased Kimura unmercifully over his habit of blithely assuming false characters on the spur of the moment, and it was with some surprise that he heard himself replying without conscious preliminary thought. "I've just come from Miyada," he said glibly. "He's worried." Over the top of Hayashi's head he saw the big foreigner's eyes narrow.

Hayashi grinned briefly, with a certain charm. "*He's* worried, is he? Dear me. He's not the only one." He glanced over his shoulder at Carradine. "Seen this man before?" Hayashi's manner was still quite equable, but Otani noted with interest that there was no evident respect in it.

Carradine shook his head. "No. Never set eyes on him." His own Japanese was plain and colloquial. It was clear that he understood and handled the language with perfect ease.

"He sent me here to talk to you both," Otani went on, improvising while trying not to be listening too obviously for the sound of oars as Migishima bore Noguchi away and arranged over the radio for reinforcements. "Can we, ah . . ." He gestured towards the cabin, whose varnished wooden door swung open behind Carradine.

Hayashi's face was now closed and wary, and he looked Otani up and down before seeming to make up his mind. "So Miyada's worried," he said, nodding slowly. "Yes. Come in here. I'd like to hear more about that."

Hayashi was wearing blue jeans with his heavy seaman's sweater, and cheap plastic flip-flop sandals on his bare feet. He was fairly obviously unarmed, and Otani had no reason to suppose that Carradine was in the habit of carrying a gun though on the other hand he was much bigger and more powerfully built than himself. The weight of the revolver in his own inner pocket was a distinct comfort. He could certainly not have hoped to hold his own against the two of them in a physical fight, but was pretty sure he had the overall advantage pending the return of Migishima with help.

When they reached the open door of the cabin Hayashi stood back and gestured to Otani and Carradine to precede him. Then he followed them in, closed the door behind him and stood with his back to it. "You," he said, pointing to Otani. "Into the corner there." Otani obediently sidled on to the bench into the position which he had seen Hayashi himself occupying earlier, and Carradine resumed his former seat, effectively imprisoning Otani behind the heavy wooden table. As he sat down, Otani glanced casually at the sheets of paper, which looked like bills of lading annotated with pencilled notes.

There was no doubt whatever about who was in charge. "Right You. What's your name?"

"Aoki," replied Otani promptly.

"I never heard of Miyada employing an Aoki before." The gaze fixed on Otani was hard and increasingly hostile.

"I didn't say I work for Miyada. I said I came from him. I'm with Yamamoto. Miyada's worried because Yamamoto doesn't like the way the last drop was bungled. Thinks Yamamoto might scrap him and cover up his traces."

Aware that he was in great danger of getting out of his depth, Otani was relieved to be given unexpected support by Carradine, whose expression had grown perceptibly more anxious during Otani's flight of fancy. He turned to Hayashi, who was still standing grimly by the door. "If that were to happen the whole thing would fall apart," he said.

Emboldened, Otani went on. "The three the fuzz picked up are rubbish," he said. "Don't know a thing. They'll go down for nine, ten years and Miyada kisses them goodbye.

"It's the end of the line for the Buchi-Buchi Angling Club, certainly," Hayashi interjected with a sour little smile.

Otani nodded seriously. "Plenty of other ways to use, though. As long as Yamamoto agrees."

Hayashi's eyes were locked on Otani's, boring into him uncomfortably. Although he had tried to coarsen his natural manner of speech to conform with his assumed role, Otani doubted very much if he could continue very long to sustain it. He was not nearly so familiar as most officers in his force with the argot used by *yakuza*, and only a few weeks before had studied with bemused interest a pamphlet circulated internally by the Tokyo Metropolitan Police Department which included a glossary of current underground terms. He now knew that he himself was probably referred to by the gangsters of Kobe as 'Daddy', and had memorised a few of the more colourful synonyms for 'woman' mainly in order to amuse Hanae. His only real hope now, though, rested in the fact that Hayashi had been out of circulation in Japan for a long time and might not be up with the latest, while Carradine, however good his Japanese, moved normally in circles where the slang of the hoodlums was seldom heard. Hayashi seemed to intuit his train of thought.

"You're an educated man, Aoki," he said thoughtfully, then whipped out the next words. "Describe the inside of Yamamoto's private office."

Otani thanked his lucky stars that he had on one unforgettable occasion been there. "Penthouse," he said easily. "Top of his office building. Done up completely Japanese style—little girl in antique kimono to bring tea—keeps his son's Navy sword and headband in the *tokonoma*." The taut suspicion in Hayashi's expression relaxed very slightly, and he nodded slowly.

It was Carradine who spoke next. "What does Yamamoto want, then?"

Otani turned his gaze on the big foreigner, and

launched on a new and dangerous tack. Migishima and Noguchi must be well clear by now, and with any luck it would take no more than another ten or fifteen minutes for help to arrive. "He wants you out of the way. They're on to you. You know that. That's why you're here now." Near as he was to Carradine, Otani could distinctly smell the man's fear. It was more than the normal 'butter stench' of all Westerners, nowadays regrettably associated with so many Japanese who had picked up their eating habits that only people of his own generation still used the expression. It was, rather, an aroma of a universal nature which Otani had detected too often in the course of his career as an interrogator to mistake.

He pressed on, aware of the tension in Hayashi also, standing as he still was with his back to the door. "You were stupid to think of getting rid of him in the first place. At least you knew who was watching you. It was even crazier to try to do it in your own home . . . and dumber still to kill the wrong one . . ." Carradine's face was drained of colour, and he seemed to be having trouble with his breathing.

"I am very very interested in what you say," Hayashi remarked evenly. "Especially since it is highly unlikely that Yamamoto has any information on this subject. On the other hand, the police unfortunately know a certain amount. Very quietly, now. Both hands high in the air, *Inspector* Aoki."

Otani cursed the fact that the all-too-solid table in front of him was bolted in place, and had to take the chance that Carradine's state of mind was such that he would be unlikely to move very fast It had been years since he had used a gun in an emergency, and months since he had last been near the basement range at headquarters. Nevertheless he got the gun into his hand with creditable efficiency at the same time scrambling up onto the bench on which he had been sitting, and from there to the table top. He felt slightly ridiculous standing there above them, but the overriding sensation was one of relief as he released the safety-catch. Keeping the gun trained on Hayashi, Otani clambered carefully down, feeling a good deal better with the bulk of the table between himself and Carradine, and the length of the cabin separating him from Hayashi.

"My turn, Hayashi," he said, panting slightly to his own annoyance. "Get behind the table. You're both under arrest." Hayashi was too fast for him. Otani was conscious only of his taking one step in the direction of the table, then he was leaping towards Otani, one sandalled foot sending the gun spinning from his hand and clattering to the floor. Otani felt his knees buckle and then he was down on his face, the younger man locking his arm in an agonising judo hold.

"Move yourself, Carradine," Hayashi said quite calmly. "Get the shooter . . ." It was at this moment that the door opened and Otani heard another, strange voice, speaking in throaty but almost apologetic tones, using words he could not understand but recognised as English.

"No, er, prease don't move, Mr Carradine. I would not rike to harm you. And, ah, Mr Rin, I think? Prease rerease Superintendent Otani." As the pressure was reluctantly reduced Otani was able to twist his head round to see a large gangling Japanese with curiously concave features beaming amiably as he stood inside the open door, a revolver rock-steady in his hand. Coming from behind him was the sound of boots and official voices. "Oh, *fuck* you, Hagiwara," said Carradine in despair to the member of the Madrigal Circle he had failed to murder.

Chapter 17

Die now, my heart

"YOU DID ALL YOU COULD," SUGGESTED AMBASSADOR Atsugi, leaning forward to refresh Otani's glass from the bottle of Jack Daniels Old Number 7 he had opened a few minutes earlier and persuaded his visitor to sample. Otani had never tasted Bourbon before, his acquaintance with whisky having been confined to domestic Japanese brands and the more popular varieties of Scotch. Otani had come spoiling for a fight with Atsugi, and although he found the smooth taste of the whisky with its hint of charcoal agreeable, he was still belligerent.

"I did," he snapped. "I wish I could say the same for your man Hagiwara. Granted I was very glad he appeared when he did, but if he'd put his damned gun away sooner Hayashi wouldn't have made a grab for it and nobody need have been hurt."

The diplomat nodded judiciously, concern in his

meaty face as he sipped at his own whisky. "It was specially ironic that it had to be Noguchi," he said. "Hagiwara heard you order him back to shore. I suppose it was his surprise at seeing him back again that made him lose his grip momentarily. It's a blessing he wasn't hurt more seriously. A nasty wound, they tell me, and a shattered rib." Atsugi sighed. "Still, he'll be able to leave hospital in a few days."

Otani put his glass down on the highly polished occasional table at his side, and stared gloomily at the expensive carpet, his hands dangling down between his knees. "Of course he was wrong to insist on coming back. But I can understand it. He was practically frantic with anxiety over his son even when he was lying on the deck with blood all over him. My wife and I are going to see him later today. I'm dreading it, quite frankly." Otani sat up straight and glared at Atsugi. "It's the same old story. You people never have the sense to realise we're on your side. If you'd told me why you had an agent planted in that wretched choir and had shared what you knew we could have cleared this whole business up in half the time." He snatched up his drink and drained the glass, then coughed and spluttered as the spirit went down the wrong way.

"I'm sorry, Superintendent," Atsugi said mildly as Otani sat back and dabbed his mouth with a paper handkerchief. "It was difficult for me to accept that somehow Carradine got wind of the fact and decided to try to do away with Hagiwara." He began to brighten as he pursued his own train of thought. "When you come to think of it, you know, it's not difficult to visualise anybody as a potential murder victim. Imagine all the excellent reasons a number of people probably have for doing away with you, for example. Or me, for that matter," he added generously. "There was that very efficient man of yours, Kimura isn't it, coming up with one perfectly well-qualified candidate after another and wrong every time. To be quite honest with you, we, um, well, as a matter of fact, we had another person in the Madrigal Circle as well . . . she'll no doubt remain a member, though poor Hagiwara will have to drop out after what's happened. A shame really, he enjoyed the weekly practices so."

"Well, you've got Hayashi. Or rather, we have." Although still greatly perplexed and troubled by what lay ahead, Otani found it impossible not to like Atsugi, and the whisky which had made him nearly choke when he swallowed it too quickly was now warming and relaxing him. He experienced a brief pang of guilt when he realised that he was due to meet Hanae in half an hour and that she would undoubtedly smell the liquor on his breath. "What are we going to do about him? Carradine is comparatively simple. We not only have a virtual confession that in attempting to bring about the death of Hagiwara by poisoning his drink he killed the woman Baldwin; but those documents in the cabin tie him in conclusively with the drug smuggling operation. We can throw all sorts of charges at Hayashi and make them stick, but it isn't a crime to be one of the most influential leaders of the Korean community in Japan, or to acknowledge his allegiance to the North. And that's all you and your Ministry care about really, isn't it?"

Atsugi waved a hand in a peacable gesture, and smiled. "My dear Superintendent, I shall begin to wonder about *your* allegiance if you speak so fondly of Hayashi. Let me remind you that he is deeply involved in drug smuggling, and that he would quite cheerfully have killed you if he had not been interrupted at the preliminary stages. It was almost certainly Hayashi who warned Carradine that he was under observation by the security services, and very probably Hayashi who obtained the *fugu* poison for him from one of his Korean associates. I hope and expect that he will be sentenced to a very long term in prison.'' His face clouded. ''Believe me, I do appreciate how painful all this must be for his father . . . Noguchi-san is of course eligible for full pension already, and if it would help, I'm sure I could arrange a generous compensation settlement in respect of the injury accidentally inflicted upon him by a member of my service in the course of duty.''

Otani felt the anger bubbling up in him anew, but succeeded in suppressing it. Atsugi was being crass and insensitive, but then he had never known Ninja Noguchi personally. From his own point of view he was trying to show understanding and even generosity. Otani shook his head and began to rise to his feet. ''Compensation, certainly,'' he said quietly. ''I doubt if money means much to him though. I simply don't know what he'll decide to do, Ambassador. I doubt somehow if he'll want to retire, though.'' He shook his head, sighing. ''I just hope he'll get over this business of his son.''

Ambassador Atsugi crossed to the door ahead of Otani and held it open for him, then accompanied him down the corridor towards the lift, one large hand resting in a friendly way on his shoulder. ''Are you going straight from here to the hospital?'' he enquired as he pressed the call button.

Otani nodded. ''Yes. My wife's meeting me at Umeda Station. We'll take the Hanshin train to Kobe.''

''Don't get lost at Umeda. I always manage to,'' said Atsugi with a smile as the lift doors opened and Otani stepped in, turned and bowed. As the lift went down, Otani reflected that although Atsugi smiled a lot, it was always with his mouth only, never his eyes.

Hanae was already waiting in the appointed coffee shop, glancing through one of the women's magazines kept for the use of customers who might well spend half an hour or so over a cup of lemon tea and a piece of cheese cake. It was a moment or two before she sensed Otani's presence and looked up at him with a sudden start. She was wearing Western dress, a plain suit in a shade of rust which she feared was several years too young for her age.

"A melon, eh?" Otani glanced at the large box on the chair at her side, wrapped in a square of plastic provided by the shop. "Have we won the Takarakuji lottery?" He sat down beside her as the waitress came over and set before him a glass of water and a little tray with a hot, tightly rolled damp towel on it. "Coffee," he said to her absent-mindedly, and she turned her head to the counter and called in English "One hot" to the young man juggling expertly with various pots and jugs behind. "I wish they wouldn't do that," Otani muttered in an irritated way. "*Wan hotto,* indeed. Why can't they speak Japanese?"

Hanae looked at him warily, and there was a defensive note in her voice when she spoke. "It wasn't all that expensive," she said. "The melon I mean. And, well, it would just seem wrong somehow to take anything else."

Otani gave her a quick smile as the girl brought his coffee and he emptied the accompanying Lilliputian jug of cream into it. "Of course. I didn't mean it."

They sat in silence for a while. He had told Hanae the previous evening as much of the story as he himself understood, having been made to promise as much when he had arrived home in the middle of the morning depressed, weary and dishevelled, with time enough only for a bath and a change of clothes before rushing back to headquarters. Over supper later Hanae had listened quietly, and at the end of the recital made just two suggestions. The first, that she should accompany him on a visit to Ninja Noguchi in hospital, he had agreed to gladly and immediately. The second, that the prisoner Hayashi should be permitted to spend a little time alone with his father, had worried Otani a lot, and he slept on the idea before finally undertaking to see what could be done.

"Well, I did it," he said at last. "Broke every regulation in the book and a few more besides. There will be a tremendous row if it comes out in any of the hearings, but we managed to give them half an hour together this morning. I suppose I could always say Ninja was taking a statement from him . . . but I don't really care anyway." Hanae discovered that she had unconsciously been holding her breath, and she now let it out gently, and surreptitiously reached for her husband's hand.

"I took personal responsibility," he went on. "He came very quietly, with Kimura and Migishima and me. There was no way I could avoid handcuffing him to Migishima during the journey to and from the hospital, but we let him go into the room alone. Afterwards he thanked me. We had a bit of a talk together, actually." Otani pushed his coffee cup brusquely to one side. "Come on, let's go," he said, and made for the cashier's desk with the bill the waitress had left, as Hanae put the magazine back tidily and gathered up her bag and the expensive musk melon in its presentation box which would shortly repose with others from wellwishers on the table beside Noguchi's hospital bed.

It was about four in the afternoon when they arrived at the entrance to the hospital, a newish building set in rather more spacious grounds than usual on the heights above the city. It was a bright, windy afternoon, and

Hanae had to hold her skirt down as she got out of the taxi which deposited them in the forecourt. Fortunately Otani was now dealing with the awkward burden of the melon. Neither of them recognised the smart young woman in fashionable but inexpensive clothes who approached, a troubled expression on her healthy, pertly pretty face, her short black hair tousled by the wind.

"It is unforgivable for me to trouble you, Superintendent," she began in the conventional way. "I am called Detective Migishima." Enlightenment came simultanously to the Otanis, and Hanae made a few appropriately congratulatory remarks about the wedding reception they had attended not so very long before. It was Otani who noted the perfunctory nature of the girl's responses and after a moment drew her aside.

After some time, Hanae saw the girl take an envelope from her bag and hand it to Otani, who opened it, took out a sheet of paper and read it with a face turned to granite. Then he very slowly refolded it, put it with the envelope in his inside jacket pocket and addressed a few brief questions to Junko Migishima, who stood stiffly to attention and seemed to answer just as concisely. Then evidently dismissed, she turned away with an air of relief, bowed awkwardly to Hanae from a distance, and was gone.

Only then did Hanae cross to Otani and study his face, standing in silence as he stared unseeingly beyond the cars parked in the hospital courtyard towards the sea in the distance. He did not look at her as he spoke. "He's dead," he said dully. "Hayashi. The son. An hour or so ago, in the cell at Ikuta Divisional Station where we took him after he came here this morning. It seems . . ." his voice broke and he had to begin again. "Seems he was high enough in the scheme of things in North Korea to have been issued with a suicide pill. Left two notes. One to me—I was just reading it. 'Non political decision', he calls it. Second note in the envelope in my pocket. Sealed. In the first note he asks if he can trust me to give it unopened to his father."

"Of course you must." Hanae's voice had a quality Otani had heard only rarely, at times when she was not to be argued with. He nodded, and moved very slowly towards the entrance to the building.

"I must tell him myself, Ha-chan," he said. "You'd better wait outside the room . . . just see him for a minute or two after . . . if he's in a fit state."

They went together into the antiseptic whiteness, and rode up to the third floor in the big lift, whose doors were wide enough to admit a stretcher on a trolley. Otani knew where to go, having been there only a few hours before, and was able to point out a place where Hanae could sit in the corridor. He seemed to be quite unaware of the melon in its box dangling by the wrapper from his hand until Hanae gently detached it and put it on the seat beside her.

After Otani tapped on the door of Private Room 361 and went in, it was twenty-three minutes by Hanae's watch before the door opened again. She was never to know what passed between the two old friends during that time, but never forgot the pain in the small twisted smile on Otani's face as he looked out and beckoned to her. "Here she is, Ninja," he said as she entered the room, "My stupid spendthrift woman, wasting my hard-earned pay on a mouldy melon for you."

There was no immediate response from the bed, but as Hanae went shyly forward and bowed very low a huge hand emerged from the snowy mountain of bedclothes and reached for hers. Ninja looked deathly pale, and unnaturally tidy, having been carefully shaved by expert hands. The sheets rose up in a majestic curve over his belly, and the blue cotton yukata he was wearing revealed the bandages covering most of his chest and one shoulder. "He can't talk very loudly," Otani explained to Hanae, who had approached the bed and was now leaning towards Noguchi, who was patting her hand and nodding almost imperceptibly.

"Look at all the loot he's got already," Otani went on in the same falsely bright voice, gesturing towards the side of the room. It was indeed a remarkable spectacle. Not only were there several melons in boxes like their own, but also two huge baskets of imported fruit covered with plastic film, and more flowers than Hanae had ever seen outside a florist's shop. One particularly enormous bouquet, magnificent in its vulgarity, had a silk ribbon attached to it bearing an inscription in bold black Chinese characters, and Otani seized hold of it. "Listen to this," he said, and read aloud. " 'Humble condolences on Your Esteemed Injury and Prayers for Swift Recovery from the Arakawa Sub-Gang Affiliated to the Yamamoto Group'. I ask you. The biggest crowd of cut-throats in the entire port area."

He was babbling and he knew it; and it was with a sense of relief that he realised that both Hanae and Noguchi were ignoring him completely, and carrying on a whispered conversation of their own. He fell silent and spent two or three minutes examining the other presents from petty crooks and small shopkeepers, among whom the news of the shooting had spread with almost instantaneous effect. Then Otani turned again to the bed, just as Hanae rose from the chair at its side and bowed again. Noguchi's eyes were open, and his expression more peaceful than before. He nodded briefly as the Otanis crossed to the door. "I'll come again tomorrow, Ninja," said Otani. "Get some sleep now."

When they were out in the air again the afternoon

was well advanced and the sun was turning from gold to red as it dipped towards the horizon. The wind had dropped, too. "Let's walk down the hill and find a taxi," Otani suggested, and made to move off, but Hanae held him back with a light hand on his forearm.

"I think Noguchi-san will be all right," she said. "At the end he told me he had discovered he has a grandson in North Korea. To carry on the good work, as he put it."

Otani shook his head ruefully, and grinned. "He's an impossible old devil," he said; and led the way out of the hospital compound and towards the bustle of Kobe below.

Chapter 18

The Curtain Drawn

KIMURA OPENED THE DOOR OF HIS OFFICE AND peeped furtively in each direction, then glanced again at his watch before emerging into the corridor. It was extremely unlikely that any of the administrative or clerical staff would be about at six-thirty in the morning, but one never knew. Then he gave a final tug at the top of his brand-new track suit, which was of a brilliant cherry red hue with white stripes by way of decoration, and made for the rear of the building.

He was fortunate. Apart from the duty riot policeman standing impassively with his long baton just outside the area where the police vehicles were garaged, Kimura passed and greeted cheerily only the bent figure of the superannuated former patrolman who pottered about most days carrying out ill-defined cleaning duties, unable to make the final break from his former profession. The guard in his blue coveralls and heavy helmet with thick plastic visor was unlikely to know who Kimura was anyway, while the old cleaner had seen much stranger sights in his time than that of a senior Inspector done up like an advertisement in a television commercial.

It had called for a great deal of effort on Kimura's part to force himself out of bed in time to shave and scramble into ordinary clothes, find a taxi and get himself and his holdall full of newly-acquired sportswear into the privacy of his office to change and be ready to join Ulla and the others at the top of Tor Road before seven, but once in the open air and loping steadily along through the practically deserted streets he felt quite pleased with himself.

It was the first of October, and it promised to be an exceptionally beautiful day. A few wisps of cloud unravelled tendrils still tinged with dawn pink high in the pale blue sky, and there was a crispness in the air which made it quite certain that the last of the summer humidity was over. Pausing obediently at a stop light and waiting to cross the main road, Kimura was mildly surprised when another jogger appeared at his side. The newcomer was an elderly man who glanced with disdain at Kimura's finery, being himself dressed in a stained vest and a pair of shorts which revealed pale, skinny legs which reminded Kimura of a plucked chicken. Kimura nodded in a friendly way at his companion, then hastily began to jog on the spot when he observed the ancient's legs still pumping up and down.

There was no sign of traffic, but they both jiggled about patiently until the lights changed, then jogged across the road where the old fellow veered off in the opposite direction from Kimura, casting a final look of suspicion at him as they parted. Kimura pressed on philosophically, past the shuttered windows of boutiques, patisseries, and bookshops with piles of magazines dumped outside, wrapped roughly in protective sheets of newspaper. He knew himself to be in good physical shape for his age, and having covered about a kilometre was congratulating himself on still breathing easily.

Then he was moving uphill, ascending the famous Tor Road with its many shops aiming specially at foreign customers. Past the expensive antique shops, the delicatessen, the Chinese and Indian tailors and the American Pharmacy, and pounding upwards with increasing speed as he caught sight of a little knot of people gathered at the far side of the broad intersection ahead. Ulla was easily recognisable by her hair and the familiar colour of her tracksuit, and he thought he could see the diminutive form of Lindy Kowalski, though she was partially hidden by a man whose back was to Kimura and who was bounding up and down on his haunches, performing professional-looking exercises. Kimura faltered and almost turned back when he caught sight of the brown beard and realised that it was Donald Schaeffer, but pressed on as he realised that the young American would undoubtedly be a great deal more shaken to see him appear on the scene.

Again the stop light was against him, and this time Kimura thankfully came to a halt. The hill had taken rather more out of him than he had bargained for, but he managed a friendly wave in response to Ulla's and had time to catch his breath and note with satisfaction the look of consternation on Schaeffer's face as he was recognised. Kimura now saw that there were two other foreigners in the group, neither of whom he knew, plus a Japanese girl whose face seemed vaguely familiar.

"Well, *hi*," said Lindy Kowalski meaningly as he finally joined the group. She looked virginally pure in her jogging gear, until Kimura came closer and observed the care with which she was made up and the depravity in the beautiful eyes which flickered up and down, taking in his appearance. "That's a really *neat* colour," she breathed.

Ulla took command, a broad grin on her face as she seized Kimura's hand and shook it firmly. "Good morning, Jiro," she said briskly. "My friend Lindy you have met: also if I do not mistake, Donald Schaeffer."

Schaeffer had once more descended to a squatting position, one leg stretched out to one side, and he glanced up awkwardly. "Yeah," he muttered. "We've met."

Without waiting for Ulla to introduce her, the Japanese girl bowed to Kimura. "I am called Mochizuki," she murmured in their own language and suddenly Kimura realised that she must be the Kumiko Mochizuki whose name had appeared on the list of members of the Madrigal Circle.

"I am glad to meet you. Please show your favour to me," he replied politely but guardedly, seizing the opportunity while her head was lowered to look quickly over her long, somewhat quizzical features. In the course of their concluding conference on the Baldwin affair, before the file was turned over to the District Prosecutor for charges to be brought against Patrick Carradine and others, as Baby-Face and the three petty crooks from the Miyada gang figured in the documents, Otani had let slip the information that Hagiwara had not been the only member of the Security Service in the group of singers.

As they both straightened up Kimura reverted to English. "Is this how you all get in training for singing madrigals, then? What with Mrs Kowalski—."

"Lindy," she said tenderly, prompting a baleful glare from Schaeffer who was now upright with his arms high above his head twisting them this way and that.

"Yes. What with Lindy here, Mr Schaeffer and now

Miss Mochizuki, well, I'm surprised you don't break into song right now."

"Not quite ready," said Ulla mysteriously. "Now you must meet Alison Jenkins and Geoff Withers."

Withers was a tall young man with an anxious manner. His track suit was a little too small for him and several inches of hairy wrist appeared as he extended his hand to shake Kimura's. "How do you do," he said earnestly, then indicated the plump but conventionally pretty young woman by his side. "This is . . . Alison." His voice dropped a tone or two as he pronounced the name soulfully, and the pair of them unexpectedly blushed brightly. It was all Kimura could do to stop himself from wishing them both every happiness so obvious was their attachment.

There was an awkward pause as they all stood about, and Kimura was about to ask what was to happen next, when Ulla uttered a relieved "Ha! At last," and turned back to the group, having been peering up the hill in the direction of the Kobe Club. "She comes, but regarding to the dog I am not so sure," she said. Kimura looked over her shoulder and his eyes widened as he saw the figure in the distance waving her arms in greeting as she bounded towards them, hampered to no small extent by the enthusiastic support of the dog Gladstone.

"Hello," she gulped as she came to a halt. "Gosh, I'm about ready to go home again, and we haven't even *started* yet. I'm absolutely *shagged*. You rotters, I thought we were supposed to meet at the Club." Mrs Byers-Pinkerton presented a bizarre spectacle, since she was dressed in an abbreviated tennis skirt under which serviceable white knickers were clearly visible. Her upper half was encased in a tight orange garment, on which was stencilled 'My Folks Went To Hawaii And All I Got Was This Crummy T-Shirt', while her hair was tied back with an acid-green ribbon. Gladstone was panting even more horribly than his mistress, and paid no attention to Kimura. He did however approach Schaeffer and cock an exploratory leg against him. Schaeffer retreated hurriedly in the nick of time.

"We usually do," Geoff Withers said apologetically. "But now we have some new friends who don't, actually, belong. I mean, to the Club, that is. What I really meant was . . ." Alison Jenkins gazed at him adoringly as he babbled into silence.

"Sorry about my clothes," said Mrs B-P, beaming round them indiscriminately without the slightest hint of embarrassment. "Thought the old tennis things would do till I decide whether I like it. *I say*, you're the sleuth! Inspector Matsuyama. Just the man I've been wanting to talk to!"

"Good morning, Mrs Byers-Pinkerton," Kimura said resignedly, still keeping a sharp eye on Gladstone. "Uh, Kimura's my name. Jiro Kimura," he said, trying not to catch Ulla's amused eye. "Good to see you, Mrs Byers-Pinkerton."

"Heavens, don't be so formal!" cried Ulla, who seemed to have emerged as the leader of the group in succession to the absent Carradines. "Let's go." She gave Schaeffer a hearty clap on the back and set off, whereupon he and Lindy followed, with the silent Alison next in close company with her admirer. It all happened so quickly that Kimura found himself in imminent danger of being stranded alone with the formidable Mrs B-P. He cast one wild look at the others who were already several yards away, and prepared to pursue them, but was arrested by an oddly forlorn expression on Mrs B-P's eager face.

"Don't go barging off like a bullet from a gun," she said. "I won't bite, you know." She was still panting a little. Kimura grinned, and gallantry broke through, especially as it began to appear that the fickle Gladstone had lost interest in him, being occupied in nosing round a crate of empty beer bottles beside the general store on the corner. "Tell you the truth," she went on, "I don't know why I said I'd come at all. Can't keep up with that lot."

"Well," Kimura suggested, "why don't we set off gently in the opposite direction and meet them on the way back?" She glanced suspiciously at him.

"Back up that hill? It'll kill me probably. But if you promise not to leave me . . . right. Tally-ho!" She took a huge breath and set off, with Kimura jogging easily at her side. Gladstone joined them with apparent reluctance, having first piddled on the beer crate.

"Do you play much tennis?" Kimura enquired after a while, when they had passed the entrance to the Kobe Club and were rounding a bend which he hoped would eventually put them on course to meet the other joggers. Her curious assortment of clothes were in sharp contrast to those of the few female Japanese tennis enthusiasts he knew, who seemed to devote more of their time and energy to matters of couture than to the finer points of the actual game.

Mrs B-P sucked in her breath with a dreadful hooting. "Not for years," she finally managed to get out. " 'Cept with kids on holiday." She pounded on grimly for another hundred metres or so, till they came to a corner, where she stopped short and pulled a face, a hand clapped to her chest. "Had it," she then announced briefly.

Kimura raised an eyebrow. He was not taken in by her obviously dramatised symptons of distress, but since the morning's jogging project had already been wrecked beyond repair, he was prepared to indulge her. "Okay," he said agreeable. "We'll just walk till we meet them. You're not far from home here, anyway."

They sauntered down the hill, in a street parallel to the one they had used in the ascent, and it occurred to Kimura that there were much less pleasant things he might be doing on such a bright and sparkling morning. This was an area of very small shops, and early as it was there were beginning to be signs of life, especially as it seemed to be the collection day for 'separated garbage', and here and there people were putting out empty jars and bottles, and piles of plastic boxes and wrappings in bags of the same material.

"What did you want to talk to me about?" he asked more for the sake of conversation than out of real curiosity.

Mrs B-P's eyes rounded. "Well, what do you think? Crumbs, we don't have excitements like the murder every day of the week, you know."

"Nothing particular to the police, ma'am," Kimura responded nonchalantly, and she looked at him with satisfying awe. "You'll appreciate I can't discuss the case with you while the matter's in the hands of the prosecutors. Still, I'd like to thank you for your cooperation." Kimura winced inwardly as he recalled the scene in the Byers-Pinkerton living room.

"Oh, that's boring," she said, pulling a face at him. "Gosh, I only lured you here to talk about it. Subject Number One for me, I can tell you, after finding out that Patrick was trying to murder me of all people . . . and out of jealousy. I ask you! Good grief, I never even knew he fancied me, let alone jumped to the conclusion that I was having an affair with poor old Fred Austin of all the unlikely lovers in Kobe." She pronounced it 'Cobey' like many foreigners, and Kimura did not at once recognise the familiar word, though this was not what caused the look of blank amazement to sweep over his face.

"I beg your pardon?"

"Oh, come on, you don't have to pretend with me," said Mrs B-P briskly. "Angela told me all about it before she left. She'll have to get a divorce of course, poor old sausage. I say, d'you reckon he'll get more than ten years?" Kimura had stopped in his tracks and was looking at her with an expression she interpreted as indicating informed interest. "Of course, you're not allowed to say," she went on understandingly.

"A moment, please. Just what did Mrs Carradine tell you?"

"She told me what happened, silly. That Patrick had gone soppy about me and thought I was spurning him. Can't say I noticed him making goo-goo eyes, but there you are, wonders will never cease. Anyway, he got hold of the idea that I was having it off with old Fred, and went bonkers. Decided I wasn't fit to live, but did poor old Dot in by mistake. Apparently he explained it all to Angela when she went to see him in jail. Anyway, you obviously know all this anyway." All at once she uttered a suppressed giggle which turned into a snort, and rummaged in her waistband until she found a crumpled paper handkerchief with which she mopped her nose. "I shouldn't laugh, I know. But I ask you! Me, a *femme fatale*. You could have knocked me down with a feather."

"Let's carry on down, shall we?" Kimura suggested carefully. "You know, I don't think we're going to meet the others, somehow. They must have gone another way."

"What? Oh, super," she said absent-mindedly. "Come on, Gladstone, you lazy old sod." They rambled on in silence for a while, as Kimura marvelled inwardly at the woman's astonishing gullibility, and wondered what extraordinary complex of motives had led Angela Carradine to elaborate such a fantasy. Could she perhaps even at that late stage have been trying to develop a line of defence which Carradine might be tempted to try on with the prosecutors, absurd though it was? Did he seriously imagine that he could somehow throw a smoke screen over the Korean drug connection?

As though she had been reading his mind, Sara Byers-Pinkerton spoke again, this time with an air of detachment. "What I don't understand is all the stuff in the paper about drugs," she said, then shrugged. "Ooh, look. Nearly home. There's the main road." Galvanised by the proximity of her house, she broke into a trot again and they rounded the corner in fine style, Gladstone lolloping at their heels. Kimura recognised where they were when she stopped at the corner of the turning which led to the Byers-Pinkerton residence.

Traffic was quite heavy on the main road now, with cars, buses and trucks streaming in towards central Kobe from the suburbs, and Mrs B-P looked even more outlandish in comparison with the soberly dressed Japanese office workers who were now to be seen here and there on the pavement on their way to work on foot.

"I say," she said conspiratorially, putting her face close to Kimura's ear. "I'd like to invite you in for a coffee, but, well, actually . . ." she went on, scarlet with embarrassment, "since all this happened, Douglas has come all over possessive and jealous."

"Please, please don't give it a thought," said Kimura hastily. "I have to get to my office now anyway."

Sara Byers-Pinkerton looked at him solemnly and nodded. "Well, I'll be off then," she said, then without warning flung both her arms round him and planted a warm kiss on his face, in her agitation missing his lips.

"I think you're a scrumptious sleuth," she muttered, then ran off, cheeks flaming.

Kimura stood in a near trance for several seconds, and did not at first hear the mild voice behind him. "I said, would you care for a lift, Inspector?" He turned round slowly and gloom suffused his being when he saw the Toyota Police Special pulled up at the kerbside, Tomita grinning from ear to ear, having quite obviously witnessed the entire episode. The uniformed figure at the back of the car was leaning politely towards the open window. Why, oh why did it have to be Otani?

About The Author

JAMES MELVILLE was born in London in 1931 and educated in North London. He read philosophy at Birkbeck College before being conscripted into the RAF, then took up schoolteaching and adult education. Most of his subsequent career has been spent overseas in cultural diplomacy and educational development, and it was in this capacity that he came to know, love, and write about Japan and the Japanese. He has two sons and is married to a singer-actress. He continues to write mystery novels starring Superintendent Otani.